DEDICATIONS

I dedicate this book to my parents Aubrey and Jacqueline Thornton. And my boys, Landon and Lance Stinnett. I would also like to dedicate this book to all the single mothers, confused black people(it's all right to love yourself),my brothers LeRoy, Larry, Aubrey, and my sister Linda. I can't forget my God-parents Joe and Corrine Montgomery thanks for all the wisdom.. And to all life's experience.

IN MEMORY OF

Sarah Ann Staten, my loving grandmother. Her spirit inspired me to start writing this book. I still feel your presence mama.

WILLIE LYNCH DOCTRINE

In 1712 a slave owner from the West Indies named Willie Lynch gave a speech to the colony of Virginia. Willie Lynch was requested by the Virginia slave owners, because they were having problems controlling the slaves at the time. Mr. Lynch had devised a plan that was guaranteed to control black slaves and it was working in the West Indies. His speech follows in it's entirety.

"The 1712 Speech By Willie Lynch"

Gentlemen:

I greet you here on the bank of the James River in the year of our Lord, one thousand seven hundred and twelve. First, I shall thank you, The Gentlemen of the Colony of Virginia, for bringing me here. I am here to help you solve some of your problems with your slaves. Your invitation reached me on my modest plantation in the West Indies, where I have experimented with some of the newest and still the oldest methods of control of slaves. Ancient Rome would envy us if my program is implemented. As our boats sailed south on the James River, named for our illustrious King whose version of the Bible we cherish, I saw enough to know that your problem is not unique. While Rome used cords of wood as crosses for standing human bodies along its old highways in great numbers, you are here using the tree and the rope on occasion.

I caught a whiff of a dead slave hanging from a tree a couple of miles back. You are not only losing valuable stock by hangings, you are having uprisings, slaves are running away, your crops are sometimes left in the fields too long for maximum profit, you suffer occasional fires, your animals are killed, gentlemen, you know what your problems are: I do not need to elaborate. I am not here to enumerate your problems. I am here to introduce you to a method of solving them.

In my bag here, I have a fool proof method for controlling your black slaves. I guarantee everyone of you that if installed correctly, it will control the slaves at least 300 years. My method is simple, any member of your family or any overseer can use it.

I have outlined a number of differences among the slaves: and I take these differences and make them bigger. I use fear, distrust, and envy for control purposes. These methods have worked on my modest plantation in the West Indies and it will work throughout the south. Take this simple list of differences, and think about them. On top of my list is "Age", but it is there only because it starts with an "A": the second is "Color" or shade, there is intelligence, size, sex, size of plantation, status on plantation, attitude of owner, whether the slaves live in the valley, on the hill, east, west, north, south, have fine or course hair, or is tall or short. Now that you have a list of differences. I shall give you an outline of action—but before that, I shall assure you that distrust is stronger than trust, and envy is stronger than adulation, respect or admiration.

The black slave, after receiving this indoctrination shall carry on and will become self re-fueling and self generating for hundreds of years, maybe thousands.

Don't forget, you must pitch the old black versus the young black, and the young black male against the old black male. You must use the dark skin slaves versus the light skin slaves and the light skin slaves versus the dark skin slaves. You must use the female versus the male and the male versus the female. You must also have your white servants and overseers distrust all Blacks, but it is necessary that your slaves trust and depend on us. They must love, respect and trust only us.

Gentlemen, these kits are your keys to control, use them. Have your wives and children use them, never miss an opportunity. My plan is guaranteed, and the good thing about this is that if used intensely for one year, the slaves themselves will remain perpetually distrustful.

Thank you gentlemen.

Forward

The real truth about Willie Lynch is very prevalent with Black people today. Why is it that we let this virus continue to perpetuate itself in our lives since it was first injected in our minds 286 years ago?. We no longer, as a Black, race have white people lynching us, we are lynching ourselves. The doctrine of Willie Lynch, evolved circa 1712, and was used as a fool proof method for controlling Black Slaves by focusing on the differences between dark-skinned and light-skinned blacks, age, gender and trust for the master.

This book depicts the social interaction between Brittany and her friends who are recent Ivy League graduates, which I will call the Buppies (Black Urban Professionals), and the BIPS, who are (Black Innercity Professionals). They have also graduated from college, but from State Colleges.

The scene is centered mostly at Venice beach. What happens when the two groups meet and discover the hatred they have for each other because of Willie Lynch's doctrine? Can these groups realize that they are all one in the same, despite the Willie Lynches which exists in their lives, or is there a real distinction among the black race?

HOW TO KILL YOUR WILLIE LYNCH

This is a story about a group of recent college graduates. Some of the graduates are returning home from Ivy League Schools, while the others have attended college locally. There is a definite distinction in economic and social class between the two groups. The Ivy Leaguers are all dark-skinned blacks whose parents have come from a second or third line of college graduates, and are all white-collar workers. The Locals are all fair-skinned blacks who are first time college graduates, and whose parents are blue-collar workers.

The time is June 15, 1996. All of the students are enjoying the summer before starting their new careers in September. The scene opens up at Venice Beach, in California. This is a popular hangout for every race, creed, color, or class of people in California. People from all over the world come here to see the diversity of California people.

The BUPPIES Characters:

Landon: 25, A graduate of Harvard University and Law School. He is engaged to be married to Brittany.

Brittany: 22, A graduate of Yale. She has a Computer Science Degree.

Kolby: 22, A graduate of Dartmouth University. She has a degree in advertising. She is Brittany's best friend.

Lance: 24, A graduate of Colombia University. He has a Marketing and Business degree. He is Landon's best friend.

The BIPS Characters:

Khari: 24, A graduate of Cal State LA. He has a degree in Engineering. He is Omunique's cousin.

Omunique: 23, A graduate of Cal State Long Beach. She has a Journalism degree. She has two children, Randolph and Jordan.

Tanika: 22, A graduate of Cal-State Dominguez Hills. She has a Liberal Arts degree. She is Omunique's best friend.

Eric-Von-Rapper: 25, A graduate of Cal State LA. He has a Business degree. He is Khari's best friend.

The Parents:

Marie: Omunique's Mom. She is an Executive Assistant.

Franklin: Omunique's Dad. He owns a trucking company.

Domunique: Brittany's Mom. She is an Attorney.

Michael: Brittany's Dad. He is a Doctor.

Katrina: Landon's Mom. She has her own Public Relations Firm.

William: Landon's Dad. An Attorney.

Randolph and Jordan: Omunique's boys.

Scene 1

Omunique: Boy, today is such a hot day. Let me put some more suntan lotion on the children so they don't burn.

Tanika: Girl, leave those children alone. They are playing so hard. They won't burn. Girl, do you think that they are white, or something?

Omunique: No, I don't think they are white. Don't be so ignorant. Black skin burns just as much as white skin. As a matter of fact, let me put some on you. You know you are getting a little red on your shoulder. We are prone to skin cancer just like they are (pointing to some white people).

Tanika: Okay, you are right. I know that we can tan even though they think we can't. I was just being funny. So chill my sista.

Khari: Hey man, turn up that song. That is the jam. I just love me some Coolio. Oh by the way, give me a dime.

Eric: Okay man, but give me twenty-five.

(all the other guys say Yo rapper).

(All the BIPS are playing dominoes talking, bar-b-queing and playing their music loudly).

(The Buppies are sitting down playing Taboo a word game, and listening to Jazz. They had their food catered).

Landon: Okay, okay Brittany you tabooed (the men to the women, we get the point).

Brittany: No, no that isn't fair. Those stupid blacks over there are acting just like niggers. They are all loud and playing that dumb low-life game. What do you call it, Dominoes or something like that? Probably can't read to play a game like this, and just listen to that mess they are listening to, rap. I bet you they are gang-bangers. I couldn't concentrate. Let's move now.

(all the other girls are shaking their heads in agreement with Brittany, except Kolby).

Landon: Hey Brittany, that is not right. You should never call another black person a nigger. We worked too hard and long to get away from that derogatory name. A nigger is anyone that is ignorant. Just because they play dominoes and listen to rap music doesn't mean they are low class, or can't read.

Lance: Yes, that's right Brittany. I've liked dominoes ever since I learned how to play at college. My ex-dorm mate came from the ghetto in Cleveland. He received a scholarship because he had a high GPA, and scored very high on his SAT exams. It has always been a black man's game. I bet all of our dad's used to play before they got so bougie, and besides, a lot of that rap music has some good information in it. Some of it is very positive. It tries to relay a message to our young black youth.

Kolby: Wait a minute Lance, you must be crazy. My daddy hasn't ever played that jig-a-boo game. And all that rap mess just talks about who's screwing who, who has the biggest butt, it degrades our women and everybody is a nigger in their song. It is awful how they glorify killing another human being. Now you can't tell me that is positive. It is actually a cause of violence.

(all the women are nodding and shaking their heads).

Lance: Brittany and Kolby you two need to stop tripping so hard. We are all black, no matter what our social economic level is. Just because some of us have not been exposed to certain things in life, doesn't mean we are bad and not intelligent. Our parents were just lucky or blessed. Call it whatever you want to, but they are the few who made it. None of us should ever forget who we are or where we came from, because believe me the others don't ever let us forget. As a matter of fact we are all just one or two generations away from where we are now.

Brittany: Boy, some of that Cleveland ghettoism must have rubbed off on you while you were away in college. Should we call you Malcolm P. whatever his name is? We don't care what you guys are saying. We are not in the same class as those blacks. Could you possibly see me dating one of them?

Kolby: My parents would kill me. I would kill myself.

Landon: His name was Malcolm X. You should read his book one day. You girls should never judge a book by its cover, and never say never. You need to look a little closer. You will find that beyond the social class you are quite alike.

Brittany: My, my Mr. Landon if I didn't know any better, I would say you could possibly date one of those round-away girls. I just know if you ever did let it cross your mind, you better not ever touch me again. Besides, look at those kids. I bet their mother had them out of wedlock. She probably is on wel-fare too.

(all the other women laugh).

Landon and Lance together: That's cold Brittany.

Landon: Girl, you actually sound like you are white. You have the nerve to put down and stereotype one of your own. You know, I took sociology last summer, and one thing that came out of it that stuck in my mind was the more we blacks assimilate with whites, the more we take on their good as well as deviant behavior. Brittany, if I wasn't standing here looking at you, I would think that you were white.

Lance: So would I. You know Brittany, Kolby, and the rest of you girls, your hair is so straight from all that perming. Oops, I mean your wigs and weaves. You all are dark, but your speech, your hair, your clothes, cars, and everything about you is shouting "I want to be white." Look at you all. You are dark and wearing blue and green contact lenses. Now you know there ain't nobody our color running around with eyes like all of yours, and blonde hair unless it was a fluke.

Brittany: Forget you Lance (all the girls chime in). What do you think? Everyone should wear their hair in an afro? Women perm their hair because it is easier to maintain than pressing it all the time. I wear my contact lenses, and my blond wig be cause it makes me look exotic, and the color looks good on my skin. I always get so many compliments. And another thing, don't down me because I speak well. Just because I don't split verbs doesn't make me bad. My parents worked too hard to get me away from the stereotypes that go with being black. So, yes, I am different and better than those types of people; and you and no one else is going to make me feel guilty because my parents were not lazy and wanted a better life for me.

Kolby: You know, this conversation sort of reminds me of that Spike guys movie. What was it called: School something? Well, you know the wanna-bees were light skinned, they were considered the elitists, but see how the tables turn. They are just yella gone to waste.

Lance: I just want to say one last thing. You know you women are considered the ones with the beauty. The media has poisoned your minds with the image of beauty. They show these white women with long, blonde hair and blue eyes and tell you this is beauty. If you ever noticed, they all want to look like you black women. They perm their hair, put pads in their butts, and inject their lips, and don't let me talk about tanning. Like my ex-college roommate would say, Lawd, have mercy, sometimes you have to look twice to make sure you are not seeing a sister when you look at them.

Brittany: (Rolls her eyes).

Landon: Okay, let's get off this conversation. I thought that we were playing Taboo.

Lance: (whispers to Landon). Man, I feel sorry for what or who you are about to marry.

BACK AT THE BIPS

Omunique: You know it is funny how things are. You would expect all of us to be doing well and to be doing what they are doing over there (looking at Ivies), because we are light-skinned. They probably are all Buppies. You know, have nice cars, go to the best colleges, and definitely live up in the hills; Must be nice.

Tanika: Yeah, it must be nice, but according to a lot of black psychologists, a lot of our so-called Buppies are very unhappy. The reason is they are trying so hard to forget that they are black. They want to fit in with the whites so badly, they lose their own identity. They start wearing colored contact lenses, perming their hair to the extreme. And a lot of times they resort to weaves and wigs, and some even go so far as trying to lighten their skin, or have plastic surgery done to make themselves look as close to Europeans as possible. I bet you Omunique, not one of those brothers would give someone like me or you the time of day, even though we are well-educated and have good morals and values. They are the kind of men who are a step away from marrying a white-woman or a woman of another race when they make it. What a waste.

Khari: I hear you girls. You are right about what you are saying. I wouldn't say all Buppie men fit the criteria, but a lot of them do. It seems that their paths have gotten crossed along the way. They don't realize a black woman is the greatest asset that they could have by their side. They can't appreciate her strength and work together to build something. They prefer to down her and get someone passive, so that they can feel like a man. Another person shouldn't have to validate your manhood. It should be there no matter what. It is unfortunate that a black man would make two children out of wedlock with a black woman, but turn around and give another woman of a different race a chance, by marrying her, and then neglect his children. Like your ex Omunique. The funny thing about it is he is a professional, but his mentality isn't. That's what I call one sorry brother.

Omunique: Thanks cuz, I feel the pain 24-7. I was supposed to take all his abuse, and not fight back. I was always the excuse for all his problems, so he says. He and his family never took responsibility for his actions. He always put me down. I know it was the right decision I made when I left. He is so full of garbage, so that is all he can give out. What's hilarious is that his wife doesn't have half, if not any of the attributes I have, but her skin is a different color, so that makes it right. She is so intimidated by me and the boys, and according to his mother the woman can't stand the fact that I had his children first. They belong together, two messed up people. You, know he told his mom the reason he married her was because he couldn't put another woman through what he put me through by having another child out-of-wedlock. Hell, he has two black boys. He should've considered coming back to me and trying to work things out with me.

(everybody: hell yeah)!!

Khari: Om, someone who deserves you and the boys will eventually come along and appreciate you, and treat you with respect. You are better off single than having that fool in your life. Give me twenty-five (all do their little hoopla).

Eric: Well, enough of that. Let's get back on the subject of the Buppies over there. Man if we were to approach one of those babes over there, they would turn their heads and noses up to us. You know, I love dark-skinned women, because I heard that they are so happy to have a high-yellow man that they treat them really well. You know they say the darker the berry, the sweeter the juice.

Omunique: Oh Eric shut up. Color has nothing to do with how a person treats you. I am a light-skinned woman and I would treat any man that I was dating wonderfully, as long as he treated me well. So now (all the women say "I know that's right").

Tanika: Well, all I have to say about this subject is a man is a man no matter what color he is. They are all after one thing, the C-A-T (All the guys bark).

Omunique: where are my boys? Girl, let me go and find them. I told them not to leave this area. Boy are they in for it.

(Calling, Randloph and Jordan's name. The boys have wandered into the Buppies area).

Brittany: Oh look at the cute little boys. They must have wandered away from their mom. Hi sweeties, what's your name? Abdula and Tupac? (all the girls start laughing, naming ethnic names).

Jordan and Randolph: (laughing together). That is not our name it is Randolph and Jordan (Brittany raises her eyebrow in shock).

Landon: Brittany, you know that is not funny. You girls are acting like real bitches. (Brittany and the girls say thank you). Why do you think that their names have to be ethnic? By the way, I have heard that a lot of the so-called ethnic names do have meaning to them(grabbing the boys hands).

Brittany: First of all, I like that I can wear the title Bitch. You know that I am a high-maintenance woman. Second, statistically speaking, all those Ghetto people or low-life usually name their children very ethnic names. Apparently, their mother had a little sense. For instance, I would name my sons some aristocratic name like Matthew, Aaron, Cameron etc. My girlfriend who is a personnel supervisor said the first thing white people look at on the resume and application is the person's name. In their little clandestine meetings, they make fun of the ethnic names and throw the applications out. I know I don't want my children to have that type of strike against them.

Kolby: That's right, Landon. I heard the same thing as Brittany. They are cute though. Hi boys (boys say hi).

Landon: Well that is just awful that we can't name our children what we would like to without them being discriminated against even more. Let me take them back to where they be long. I'm pretty sure their mom is getting worried. Come on boys, show me where your mom is.

Omunique: (walks up). She address the boys without looking up at Landon. Didn't I tell you boys not to leave the area. Why did you leave?

Randolph: Jordan kicked the ball over here, and I came to get it.

Jordan: It was an accident, mommie.

Landon: I was just getting ready to bring them back. They are very handsome young men. I can see why. (all the while he has been mesmerized by her beauty).

Omunique: (Looks up. She is startled by his good looks. The boys are playing next to their mom). Why thank you for the compliment (blushes). I'm sorry for the inconvenience . We were talking and I wasn't paying attention to them. They usually do what I say.

Landon: Well, children will be children.

Omunique: Yeah, I guess you are right. You must have some.

Landon: No way, not until I have been on my job for a little while and buy some property. I just graduated from Yale Law School. My fiancee says we have to wait until the time is just right.

Omunique: (looking disappointed). Oh, well sometime plans just don't work out the way we want them to.

Landon: What about you and your husband?

Omunique: Well, I'm not married. I just graduated from Cal-State. I will be working for a major network as a newsreporter. My major was journalism. My children's father is a corporate attorney. He felt his career came before any children, with his sports car being second.

Landon: That's too bad. He will regret it one day. He has two very fine young men, not to mention the mother. You never miss your good thing until it is gone.

Omunique: Oh cut it out!! (blushing) You sound just like a cajoler.

Landon: No, I just call things the way they are.

BACK TO THE BUPPIES

Brittany: (to group) Landon, sure is talking to that sleaze-bag a long time. I bet she is just dying to get someone like him to be a father for her babies. Just let her kids run wild. Let me walk over and check it out.

Kolby: Yeah, I think you better. I heard those yellow women move really fast. Take your man from you right under your nose; Never knew what hit you. They know how to work it (Moving her hips) you know what I mean?

Brittany: Shut-up Kolby!! First of all, Landon, wouldn't be interested in a girl with children, and secondly, she is not even in his league.

Lance: She sure is fine, and if those are her two children, she looks good for having babies. She is a red-bone too (all the guys remark how fine she is).

Brittany: Screw all you guys. Landon knows where his honey comes from. She is not any competition.

(BACK TO LANDON AND OMUNIQUE.)

Landon: Well, I hope you enjoy the rest of the day here at the beach. By the way, my name is Landon, and yours (extends his hand).

Omunique: My name is Omunique (takes his hand).

Landon: Wow, Omunigue and that you are. Your name is so appro.po.

Omunique: There you go again (blushing).

Landon: Well, maybe our paths will cross again in the future(still holding her hand). You never know.

Omunique: (still holding his hand). You never know.

Brittany: (walks up). Hi Landon, is this the kid's mother?

Landon: (abruptly takes his hand away). Oh yes, this is Omunique. Omunique, this is my fiancee, Brittany.

Omunique: I was just thanking him for bringing the children back (extending her hand to Brittany to shake it. Brittany doesn't put her hand out to accept).

Brittany: Well, you and your husband should keep a better eye on your kids. You are married, aren't you? They shouldn't be running around like that.

Omunique: You're so right (glaring at Brittany) we will make it a point to do just that.

Brittany: (turns and starts walking away, pulling Landon's arm). Come on Landon, everyone is waiting on us to finish playing Taboo.

Landon: Okay. Bye Randolph and Jordan.

Randolph and Jordan: Bye, Mr. Landon.

Omunique: Go on boys I will race you back (the boys run off, and she walks slowly, as she says to herself) I just let her make me feel like shit. Probably thinks that all people out of her class have children out-of-wedlock.

Brittany: Landon, I bet she wasn't married; probably had those children out of wedlock. You notice she didn't respond to my question when I said "you're married, aren't you?"

Landon: Stop pre-judging people. Just because someone has children out-of-wedlock doesn't mean that they're bad people. Some people just make wrong decisions when they engage in sex. Besides, you would've had a few too, if you hadn't had those abortions; because I definitely wasn't ready for marriage at the time. Does that make us bad people?

Brittany: How dare you bring that subject up? It sounds to me that you are defending that girl. At least I made the right choice instead of bringing another statistic into this world. You want that yellow trash or something? You sure were over there for awhile talking to her, and buddy I saw you yank your hand from her when I walked up. You just better be cool buddy, because the day I hear or see you with a low-life you're out of my life.

Landon: Wow, where did all this come from? I don't even know the girl. I just met her and talked for a brief second. I will never see that girl again(in his mind he is hoping that he will).

Brittany: Well, you just better make damn sure you don't.

Omunique: (arrives back with her friends looking down).

Tanika: (Coming over to meet Omunique) Hey girl, I saw you over there talking to that tall dark and handsome man. Did he try to rap to you? Hey what's wrong. I can see it all over your face. What happened over there?

Omunique: Oh it's nothing. I was talking to him because he was bringing the children back. He told me that he just graduated from Yale Law School and that he's engaged. His name is Landon. Well, while we were saying good-bye, his fiancee walked up, and acted like I was some piece of trash. "She said that my husband and I should keep a better eye on my kids", then she said, "you are married aren't you?"

Tanika: Why that little bitch You know what Dr. O.C. always says in church; no one can make you feel bad about yourself unless you let them. You are just as good as she is, even though she went to some Ivy League school and is a buppie. It all depends on your consciousness level. I also told you about feeling bad about having children out-of-wedlock. God blessed you to have two healthy, beautiful black men, who will one day make you very proud. You are doing a wonderful job with them. Just because that fool wasn't man enough to work things out with you, and appreciate what he had, don't let him win anymore. He put you down all the time when you were with him. You look better alone than you did when you were with him. You gave him the power to take away all your self-esteem. You've just about regained it all. Don't lose it again because of what that girl said. Whenever you have to put others down, that means that you don't feel good about yourself. You love yourself the way you are. I will keep repeating this until the end, because I see your shining star behind all your tears and faults. Now get it together before we walk over to the others. Anyway, you know how clairvoyant I am. I think brother man kind of liked you. I feel it deep down in my bones. You will meet again. I am sure he saw your shining star. He gave you some of his energy.

Omunique: Thanks T. I needed that. I am a good person, and I can have a man like him in my life. I am deserving. Yeah, right.

Khari: (walking over hears conversation). Hey girl, stop tripping over that man. All he sees is a nice looking woman with children, who he can possibly take to bed. He can't see past that, because most men think that women with children need them, so they tend to play games. All this shit about they don't want a ready-made family, but yeah, they can make ready-made families and leave them for someone else to raise. He thinks that he is too bougie for someone like you.

Tanika: Damn you, Khari. Now you know that was a mean thing to say. Om is just as good as those high class-broads, if not better. Besides, it's what's on the inside not the outside of a person that truly counts. I wouldn't want anyone who couldn't see that. Of course, looks are the first thing that attracts you to someone, but what happens after the looks? Another thing, her having children doesn't limit her chances, of finding a good man unless she believes it will. My cousin married into a very wealthy family. She has three girls. That man and his family worship the ground my cousin walks on. At first, they all protested, now they say he couldn't have found a better person. So once we get off all the superficial things about people, we can all live a more enlightened life.

Eric: (walks over and overhears a conversation). Khari is not saying that it's not impossible for Om to meet and marry a man like Mr. Buppie or anyone else. He is just saying that it takes a good man to love and respect her as a person and not as a liability. She is very attractive, sensitive, spiritual, independent, educated, and a darn good mother. She would be an asset to any brother.

Omunique: (hugs Eric). Why thank you my brother. You guys enough already. I never said I wanted to marry the guy. I just said he seemed nice, and I wouldn't mind dating someone like him. Besides what any of you say, I am more of a liability than an asset. How many men really want a ready made-family?

Tanika: Well, you keep thinking that way, then it will be. As O.C. says, a man is what a man thinks. Don't let your thoughts become a reality. There is a good man out there for you and the boys. We all know it; now you've got to believe it yourself.

Omunique: I am really trying to. Hey, are you guys ready to get going? It is starting to get a little cold out here.

Back at the Buppies

Lance: I saw you talking to that fine red-bone. Were those her children? You know that is something you just hit and get out..You don't want to get serious with someone with children. I can just see your parents passing out if you brought her and her children home. (laughing). Guess who all are coming to dinner?

Landon: Man shut-up! Just because women have children, doesn't make them less of a woman. It really wouldn't bother me if I did marry a woman with children. As far as my parents, they can't live for me. They must accept anyone I decide to be with. I am my own man. You know, it's funny how we pre-judge our own people. I just knew that she was going to be the lip-smacking, neck turning black woman with bad grammar. She was just the opposite; very intelligent, just graduated from college here locally, and will be working for a major network in September. I think she was possibly irresponsible. It is unfortunate that our society has a double standard for men and women. The man can make all the babies he wants, and leave the woman with the responsibility, and start a whole new life over with a new woman. Nobody looks at him as having a ready-made family. I just hope, at least, the brother is paying child support. After all, she said he is a corporate attorney. He felt his career was more important than her and the children. Who says education makes us smarter than the average Joe Blow on the streets? A lot of times it makes us act colder towards each other.

Lance: Wow! Landon, how did you find out so much information that quickly? Man, I can see it in your eyes and hear it in your voice. She actually moved you. I know you man. You wouldn't take the time with a person unless you are interested. I made one comment and you are ready to jump all over me. You know a lot of things you said about women with children are exactly right. I never looked at it that way. I would hate for someone not to like me just because I had children.

Landon: Well, to be frankly honest, I saw something genuine and unique in her. It is ironic her name is Omunique, and that she is. I was just getting up the nerve to ask her could we keep in touch, then Brittany walked up. Brittany tried to put her down, as she usually do with people. Man, I haven't had this feeling about a woman in years. I hope that our paths will cross again. Boy, if I only knew her last name.

Lance: What is this I am hearing? You are starting to see Brittany for who she really is. I know I've been trying to tell you for years that you deserve better. Who knows what might happen? You may actually get the opportunity to meet your Cinderella again. It happens all the time in fairy tales, but all joking aside, if it's meant to be, you will run into her again.

Landon: Lance, I have always seen Brittany for what she really is. It's just that our parents have arranged this marriage since we were little. They act like we're in the Middle East or something. They claim they want to keep the money in the family, and that you marry people in the same class as you are, so, in other words, I've learned to accept Brittany, and say Que Sera Sera. Love has nothing to do with this relationship. While I've been away at college, I've realized that I can't live for my parents. I just haven't figured out a way to tell Brittany and my parents. When the right time comes, I guess I will do it.

Lance: Man, I'm really proud of you. You have finally come into your manhood. You know my parents feel the same way yours feel about marrying out of your class, but to me that is Bunk!!, I will marry whomever makes me happy. They say that I am a rebel and have always been since I was a child. Love is where you find it, not them finding it for me. I just want you to know Landon, that I am by your side with whatever decision you decide to make (they give each other a hug).

Brittany: Hey you guys, I am getting cold, let's go. My hair is starting to frizz up.

Kolby: So Brittany what happened over there? Was she trying to get your man?

Brittany: Of course she was. She would love to have a man like him to take care of her and her children. Little Jezzy-belle...

Kolby: Now Brittany, you don't even know the woman. Do I detect a hint of jealousy in your voice? (all the girls start saying um hum).

Brittany: First of all, she is no damn competition, and no, I'm not jealous of some piece of yellow-trash like her. My man would never in his life be interested in someone like her. I must admit though, she surprised me. She spoke very intelligently, and replied very tactfully to a statement I made. I was expecting her to start rolling her neck and put her hands on her hips.

Kolby: Just goes to show us that all low-lifes are not ignorant and not unintelligent. Maybe we better check ourselves. The more I think about it, who are we to judge someone else? Our parents just happened to be the select few who've made it. I couldn't imagine how it would feel if they were us and we were them. It's funny, now I am beginning to understand what my black history teacher was trying to teach us. I thought he was just tripping. He often said that whites have used color, class, and economics since slavery to divide and exploit us. I see it with what we are doing now with those other blacks. He use to also say that no matter how much money we make, we are still black in the white man's eyes, and unless we come together we are a doomed race.

Brittany: What's wrong with you Kolby? Taking black history in college?

Kolby: I needed one more elective to graduate and that was the class that was open, so I decided to take it. Matter of fact, I kind of enjoyed it.

Brittany: Well, you would've never caught me taking a class like that, and about that statement you made about how whites see us. I know they don't see me the same way as they see them(pointing). I'm always told that I'm different from other blacks. You know you are scaring me. You are starting to sound like Landon and Lance. If only your mother heard you say what you just said, she would probably faint. We are different. We don't have children out-of-wedlock. We don't act loud and obnoxious out in public. We speak very good English, and we have a lot going for ourselves. If you want to see how much different we are from them, try bringing one of those low life boys home to meet your parents.

Kolby: You know, I am tired of this whole conversation. And another thing, I made up my mind before I graduated that I was going to be with whomever made me happy. I have tried my parent's way all my life. Now I will be starting my career and paying my own bills, they can't tell me how to live my life anymore.

Brittany: We will see (Landon and Lance walk over to help gather up everything).

(Scene ends with both groups getting into their cars).

Scene 2

(Khari drops Omunique and children off at home).

Omunique: Come on Randolph and Jordan (both are sound asleep).

Khari: Hey cuz, let me help you carry the boys in.

Omunique: Thanks Khari. It's nice to have a cuz like you. (They take the children into the house, take off their shoes, and put them to bed).

Khari: See you all at church tomorrow.

Omunique: Okay, but save me a seat if you get there before me.

Khari: Yeah right, just don't take all day(kisses her on the cheek). Good night. Om, don't worry about a man. God will send you a good man and father for your children.

Omunique: Thanks Khari, drive safely. (Om prepares the children's clothes for church tomorrow. She begins to talk to God while the radio is playing. The song "Somewhere there's a Love Just for me." (where) Lord it gets very hard being a single mom sometimes. I don't know the reason you choose to let me be this way, but I know you do. I love my boys with all my heart and wouldn't give them back for anything in this world. Sometimes, I feel just like giving up, but you always give me that extra push to keep on going. I just wish that you would send someone to help me, and love me and be a good father and husband. I don't know why but Landon is staying on my mind. I was really moved by him. I felt something really genuine about him. Please let our paths cross again and I hope that he feels the same about me.

(Landon drops Brittany off and kisses her very lightly goodnight).

Brittany: Don't be late picking me up for church tomorrow Landon, and don't forget everyone is going to brunch after church to celebrate.

Landon: Awe right, Britt. Well, have a nice night, Britt. (After Brittany gets out,Landon starts thinking about Omunique. The song "Be my Girl" is playing on his car radio. The line about "your brown eyes converted me is playing". Landon starts singing along). Boy, I hope I run into her again.

Scene 3

(The next morning Omunigue is rushing to get the boys ready for church. The phone rings, it's her mother wanting to know what time she and the boys will be at church. She also tells her that the brunch reservation was confirmed yesterday).

(Landon is walking out the door telling his parents he is on his way to pick up Brittany. He will see them at church).

Scene 4

(Rev. O.C. is making an announcement about all the graduating students. He first announces all the BIPS: Omunique, Tanika, Khari, and Eric. He announces what they will be doing in September in their careers. He then welcomes all the graduates who were away at school. Landon, Lance, Brittany, and Kolby. He also announces their careers for September. Everyone is standing up while the congregation is applauding. At the end, he makes a special announcement that Brittany and Landon are engaged).

Omunique: Tanika, look over there!, Oh thank you God, you heard my prayers. I can't believe it. That's that guy Landon I met at the beach yesterday. Wow, is he ever fine!!

Tanika: You are right he is. Girl, he looks even better in a suit. Didn't I say that you would run into him again. I just know these things. I actually felt it and my hunch is never wrong. Girl, check out his friend. I wouldn't mind meeting him. He's probably engaged too.

Landon: Lance, check it out. Look over there, it's Omunique; the girl I met yesterday at the beach. Can you believe it? This has got to be fate. I have to get her number somehow.

Lance: Man, that's your Cinderella. Didn't I say if it was

meant to be, it would happen. Nothing is coincidental. Check out her friend. You must introduce me to her.

Kolby: Brittany, do you see what I see? It's that girl with the children who we saw at the beach yesterday.

Brittany: Those low-lives, what are they doing at a church like this? This church is for the elitist.

Kolby: Brittany, don't start in church. Church is supposed to be for everyone. It has no race, creed, color, or class. I came here to get a blessing and you are not going to stop me from getting it.

Khari: Man that girl Brittany is fly. I wish I could meet her.

Eric: I was too busy checking out her girlfriend. But you and I know neither one of them would give a brother like us a chance.

(Everyone is seated now. Rev. O.C's sermon is "No one person is better than another." A lot of negative things which Brittany has said about people is in his sermon).

(Brittany is trying to keep from crying), however she is so stubborn she is not changing her opinion. She utters under her breath, "Yeah right.")

(After church everyone is getting into their cars to go to brunch).

Scene 5

(Everyone arrives at Henry's a very Boogie type of black-owned restaurant. The owners are a successful black actor and a ex-basketball player among several others black owners).

Omunique's mom: (Marie) I am so proud of you. You all come on and sit down. (She kisses Om, Eric, Tanika, and Khari. All the other parents kiss them also. Marie takes Randolph and Jordan and puts them in their seats).

Omunique's dad: (Franklin) What are you kids doing today?

Khari: We're going to hang out at the beach again. We are going to play volleyball.

Marie: That's nice. Om, why don't I keep the children for you today? You can consider my deed one of your graduation presents. You know I don't keep children.

Omunique: That's great Mom, cause I know how you feel about baby sitting. Boys, would you like to go with your grandparents?

Randolph and Jordan: (together) Yeah grandma.

(The Buppies enter the restaurant, not seeing the BIPS).

Tanika: Don't look now, but the man of your dreams just walked in.

Omunique: (turns and looks) I can't believe it. This must be fate. Here I meet this guy yesterday at the beach thinking I would never run into him again, and I have already run into him twice.

Marie: Hey, aren't those the kids that graduated from all those Ivy League schools that O.C. announced today? Which one are you attracted to Om?

Omunique: The tall, dark handsome one. He brought the children back to me when they ran off yesterday. He was extremely nice.

Marie: Well, he looks really nice. Didn't they announce his engagement today in church?

Omunique: Yes, they did. He also told me he was engaged when I met him, but I got this feeling something wasn't right. Call it wishful thinking, but my intuition about something is usually right.

Marie: Well, the way that woman is holding on to him, I don't think he will be going anywhere. A nice man will eventually come along in your life, Om. Just keep praying (she kisses her daughter's fore-head).

Landon: (sees Omunique, and gently pulls away from Brittany and whispers to Lance). Lance would you look at that, Omunique is here. This has got to be fate. Man I have to find a way to get her number before we leave here today. We may have to work out a plan.

Brittany: (sees the BIPS). Well, well look at who we have here, the low-lives. Boy, they seem to get around. I wonder what they are doing at a place like this? They are trying to move up in the world. Well, we know that they are college graduates from State schools, so maybe they are trying to better themselves, but like they say: You can take the people out of the Ghetto, but you can't take the Ghetto out of the people: Oh, there's Mom and everyone!!

Kolby: Didn't you hear anything Rev. O.C. said today?

Brittany: Oh hush, Kolby, this place is going to the slums now. I won't be visiting it anymore!

(Landon and Lance look at each other and shake their heads at Brittany).

(Both groups are laughing and talking. Landon can't keep his eyes off of Omunique).

Omunique: Excuse me, I need to go to the restroom.

Landon: (realizes that Omunique has gotten up). Uh, excuse me you guys, I really need to go to the restroom. (at the hallway of the restroom, Landon cuts Omunique off just as she is getting ready to go into the women's room). Hey, what a coincidence we meet again. I couldn't believe it when I saw you in church and now we meet again. This must be my lucky day. You look extremely nice in clothes.

Omunique: (blushing) Why thank you, so do you. I was rather surprised also. I presumed you and your family are members of City of Wings.

Landon: Yes, and I presumed you are too. Congratulations for graduating.

Omunique: Yes, we are, and thank you. I believe I owe you two congratulations; graduation and engagement. Well, you take care and have a nice life (she pushes the door to go into the restroom).

Landon: Wait, Omunique. I figured since we keep running into each other like this, that it must be fate. I would like to take you and the boys out to dinner to celebrate our graduations, if you don't mind?

Omunique: Oh, I guess we could celebrate your engagement at the same time? Landon, I appreciate the gesture, but I don't go out with engaged or married men. Do you think I am desperate for a date or something?

Landon: No, I don't think you are desperate. And about my engagement, things are not always what they seem to be. You should know that, Ms. Journalist. My engagement was arranged since I was small. Our parents are part of this elitist black club called Harry and Jane. Please have dinner with me and I will explain everything.

Omunique: Listen, I don't want to hear any sob stories. You guys always do that when you want to take someone out, especially married men: The line is always the same. I don't love, her but I stay with her because of economics or the children. Spare me the drama.

Landon: Omunique, I am being very sincere. Can I please have your telephone number? I was really moved by you yesterday. There is something very unique about you. I would give you mine, but I don't want to miss an opportunity to get to know you better. You would probably never call. Would you please just take a chance and trust me?

Omunique: Well, I was kind of moved by you yesterday too. I usually don't give married or engaged men my number, but I am going to step out on faith. The truth will always reveal itself. It is 310-555-1212. Can you remember it?

Landon: I told you I never leave anything to chance (He pulls out his electronic planner, punches her number in).

Omunique: Well, I better get back. Everyone probably thinks that I've fallen into the toilet. By the way, I don't take my children out on my dates with me. I don't think they should be exposed to my dates until I know it is going to be something serious.

Landon: I can appreciate that, so that means you will go out with me?

Omunique: We will see.

Landon: So how are you going to enjoy the rest of this beautiful day?

Omunique: Well, we are heading back out to the beach for volleyball, and I think the Black Ski Club is having their party today.

Landon: Hey, that's where we're heading today also!! Hopefully, I will see you there. How lucky can a man be?

Omunique: Oh quit it!!

Brittany: It's sure taking Landon a long time. He must of had to take care of some serious business in there.

Lance: (noticing that Omunique is gone too), Oh, I think he said his stomach was killing him from something he had eaten yesterday at the beach. (he notices Brittany is about to turn around and if she does she will notice that Omunique is gone too). Hey Brittany, what are you going to have?

Landon: (walks up) hey, has everybody ordered yet?

Lance: Boy, that pâte you had yesterday at the beach really got to your stomach. I was just telling Brittany how sick you said you were.

Landon: Oh yeah, man, everything just came out.

Landon's mom: (Katrina) Are you all right, son? You sure you want to eat something?

Landon: Yeah mom, I am alright. It all came out in the bathroom.

Brittany: How gross, Landon. Well, I was beginning to wonder if something had happened to you.

Landon's dad: (William) Well son, hurry up and look at the menu. I'm hungry.

Landon: Okay Pops.

Brittany's mom: (Dominique) Well Katrina, when do you want to get together to start planning the wedding? You know it has to be the wedding of the century. We have to notify Airplane Magazine in time for the society page.

Katrina: Well, the kids haven't given us an exact date yet. Landon, do you and Brittany know approximately when you want to get married?

Landon: No, not yet Mom. I just graduated and I have to study for the bar, while working. Let me handle first things first.

Brittany: Well, I want to do it by December, because I want to have a Christmas wedding.

Landon: Well Brittany, I don't know. That may be too soon. I was thinking about sometime next year.

Brittany: Are you crazy, Landon? I am not waiting another year.

William: Hey you kids, no need to start arguing about the wedding now. You two get together and come up with a date. It seems to me that you two haven't been communicating. What do you think, Michael?

Brittany's dad: (Michael) Well whatever you say, William. I don't really care when, because I am the one who is going to be footing the bill(laughs).

Kolby: Enough about marriage. Let's hurry up and eat, I don't want to miss the Black Ski Club party.

BACK AT THE BIP'S TABLE

Tanika: Girl, you sure were gone for a long time. I noticed that Mr. Tall, dark, and handsome was M-I-A too. You guys were talking, weren't you?

Omunique: Well, matter of fact, yes we were. He asked me to go to dinner with him and for my number. At first I said no, because you know how I feel about dating engaged or married men. He said things are not what they seem, and that the marriage was arranged since he was small. He wants to explain it to me.

Marie: Om, I don't want you to get hurt so be careful. A lot of times, men will say what they think you want to hear. They are those so-called, uppity blacks, and they would look down on someone outside of their economic realm. They try to act like they are not black, arranging their kid's marriage. They want to keep that so-called nouveau money in the family. It is just another way we divide ourselves. It is just like some people from New Orleans who want to keep that light skinned blood in their family. They call themselves Creole. It shows their ignorance, because Creole is a culture not a race; but they believe that it makes them better than regular blacks.

Eric: You know Ms. Marie, you are so true. We're our own worst enemy. The white man loves for us to have this separation. I've heard tell that it's some kind of Willie Lynch syndrome-blacks against blacks or something. I know there is strength in numbers, and if we all stop tripping, and come together our people could be powerful. We are the most talented, most entertaining, smartest, and strongest race of people. Think about it. Our ancestors, who survived the passage over here, had to be all of these things for us to be sitting here today. They knew how to survive.

Omunique: Well, you all don't have to worry about me. I am a big girl. I can take care of myself, and I've been around long enough to discern who is playing a game with me.

Tanika: Well, make sure he doesn't try to just use you as his humping bag.

Omunique: Now Tanika, you know me; so that statement was not necessary.

Khari: All she is trying to say Om, is that Mr. Buppie might be trying to take advantage of a situation. You being a single-mom, and him being the man with the money. He might think that you need him and offer to do things for you and the boys, but would never take you home to mommie.

Omunique: I just don't get that impression of him. But, I will keep my guard up.

Franklin: Come on you guys, lets order and eat. The children are getting restless.

Scene 6

(Everyone has arrived at the beach. It is jammed packed because every year the Black Ski Club has their party there. Om and her friends are playing volleyball, so are Landon and his friends).

Lance: Hey look, it's our so-called rivals over there playing volleyball. Why don't we go over and play against them. They look like they may be some competition,(Everyone says all right).

Brittany: No way. I will not play against them. If we lose, they may kick our butts or something.

Kolby: Get real, Brittany. Now we have seen that they belong to the same church we do,eating at the same types of places we do, and are educated. We shouldn't pre-judge anymore. I say let's go and play against them. I think that it would be fun. (everyone says yes).

Brittany: Well I am not going to play with those low-life people. Don't come crying to me when they kick your butts.

Landon: Brittany, I am so tired of your remarks. You need to take a black awareness class. You know what I learned being in college at an Ivy League School? No matter how much we make it in life, we are still black in the white man's eye. Yeah, I thought the same way as you do before I went away to college. We went to the best schools, lived in the best neighborhoods, ate the finest foods, and drove the best cars. Our English was impeccable and we had more than enough spending money. Once I got out there in the real world reality set in. I had to study twice as hard as my other class-mates, because no matter what I turned in, the professors didn't like it. I would read my white classmates material and it wasn't half as good as mine. I couldn't understand. I started feeling like I was inferior, and I had never experienced this feeling before. It just so happened some of my class-mates saw I was getting a bum rap, and they knew what was going on even though it was unspoken. They took me under their wings and provided me with exams and materials that had been passed down all the way from their great, great grandfathers who had attended the college. Here, I was busting my butt and studying for weeks to prepare for the test, and I always wondered why I never saw them studying. They made it seem very easy. Then I realized that they had material which I could had never had access to. I am a second generation college grad in my family. It was then I realized that I am just a black man in a white man's world. I'm not saying that I don't appreciate all that my parents have done for me; it's just that reality hit me hard in the face. I just know who I am now and where I am going, and when you put one of us down, you are putting us all down.

Brittany. First of all Landon, you have changed a lot since you have been away at school. I have been seeing it all along, but I thought that you would grow out of it. Yeah, we all experience some hard times, but we are different from your average blacks. Weren't you the one who said at one time that you could never be around any low-life blacks and "Unless they came from the same class that you did and had some money, all they could do for you is to shine your shoes?"

Landon: Yes, I guess I did, but I was in the dark then. I now see the light. I just want you to wake up, before it is too late.

Brittany: Landon, Landon, Landon, I don't care what you say I am different. I am not like those low-life blacks. In school, my white friends treated me like I was one of them. My values are totally different. Blacks have children out-of-wedlock and then go around looking for fathers for their babies, then get on welfare. I wasn't raised to think that way. I soar with eagles and I am not about to lay down with dogs and get fleas. (everyone starts shaking their heads in disgust at Brittany). So, don't try and lay a guilt trip on me.

Landon: Brittany, we have already discussed the issue about women having children out-of-wedlock. Don't let me go into it again. Never judge a person until you have walked in their shoes. Another thing, all un-wed mothers are not on welfare either. You don't know the dynamics of what went on in a relationship for a person to choose not to have an abortion and elect to keep a child.

Lance: You know, Landon is totally correct in everything he has been saying. We are no better than any other blacks, because we are fortunate enough to have the finer things in life. We are a very small minority who have made it. We all need to come together. I am tired of playing the white man's game all the time. I have to talk white, think white, act white. Sometimes I actually forget that I am black. I have to look in the mirror at times to remind myself. Maybe you should start doing that more often Brittany. What you see, is exactly what they see, unless you have fooled yourself so much, that the image you see in the mirror isn't really yours.

(everyone says oooh).

Brittany: Lance, you are ignorant!! I don't have to listen to anything you are saying. You think that you are the authority on blacks. You are the one who probably has Landon thinking like he does now, just because you roomed with a so-called homey.

Landon: No, he isn't Brittany, I am my own man. And since we are talking about me being my own man, I may as well tell you now how I really feel.

Lance: Landon, man, now is not the time. Please, not now, trust me.

Brittany: Now is not the time for what? What are you talking about Landon? What have you done now?

Landon: It is nothing, Brittany. I was just talking off the top of my head.

Kolby: Well, I do have something I would like to say on this topic, since a can of worms has been opened. I am sorry, Brittany. What the guys are saying is right. You know it too. Remember how hard it was for you to pledge that all-white sorority? You called me crying about how prejudiced they were, and how you felt like a token black, because they made all types of racial remarks. They made you dress up like Aunt Jemima and serve them all pancakes when you were on line. You said how they all teased you about your hair, and made you wear pig-tails for two whole weeks to school. And oh, don't let me forget about the clubs that they never invited you to. You used to call me and cry, because you were stuck at home a lot of weekends. It was then that I realized that we were no different than any other blacks out in the world. I didn't pledge the white sorority because I would not and could not do the things you did to get in.

Brittany: Kolby, you little bitch. You promised me you would never mention any of this to anyone. I thought that you were my friend. How could you. Well, yes, all right I did everything to get in, and I am glad I did. Look at my ring, I am an ACA Soro.

Kolby: I am your friend. That's why I think it is time for us all to stop fooling ourselves. If you noticed, no contact lenses or wigs today. I am a black woman with brown eyes. I stopped wearing them a long time ago, because I wanted to be me. I started wearing them this summer only around you all, because I wanted to be accepted. I didn't know that just about everyone of you got a reality check while you were away at college too.

Landon: You lied to me Britt. You said everything was just hunky-dory up at college, and that you had no problems with pledging the sorority. I would have never let you go through with it if I had been there.

Brittany: Well, you were not there. The fact is, I made it. I am the first black that has ever made it. I feel privileged.

Kolby: Yeah, you should, Ms. Token

Brittany: Kolby, toke it up. You are just jealous. Besides, you look like shit today. You look just like a jig-a-boo. You will never catch a man looking like that.

Landon: Okay, okay, I am tired of this conversation. Some people will never change. I want to go and play volleyball with them. Who ever wants to come is welcome to come. I hope that you reconsider, Brittany. By the way, Kolby, the guys and I were just talking about how good you look today. We couldn't believe it was you. You have been hiding all this beauty for a long time. Some man is going to be lucky.

Kolby: Why thank you Landon, and I know you never tell a lie. I feel good too.

Brittany: Yeah, right. (starts laughing).

Lance: Hey, while you guys were over here deciding if you were going to play or not, I went over to challenge them to a game. They were cool and said come on over (everybody starts running over. Brittany stays behind).

Landon: Come on Britt, let loose and have some fun

Brittany: No, someone needs to be here to watch our things. I want to sit here and check out this C.D. anyway.

Landon: Well, I don't think anybody would bother our things. We are less than 25ft. away, and somebody can always be watching. But if you decide to change your mind, you know where we are.

Scene 7

(Everyone is introducing themselves to each other. They all proceed to play volleyball).

Brittany: (sitting, watching everyone playing V-ball. She starts talking to herself: "I don't ever want to be considered a low-life black person. If I start hanging out with those types of people I may start speaking ebonics like them, and start acting like them. Oh boy! My parents struggled too hard to get away from the stereotypes of black people. Sometimes though, I wish it didn't have to be this way. I wish that I could relax and enjoy life, but I can't. I have to act white to make it in our society and nothing and no one is going to keep me from achieving my goals.")

(Khari has just taken a break and asked someone to fill in for him. He sits down and picks up his Malcolm X book. He notices Brittany sitting alone. He figures this is his opportunity to meet her. He walks over towards her. She sees him coming towards her and starts to get real nervous).

Khari: Hey, I am not going to bite you. My name is Khari, and I noticed you were sitting over here by yourself. Is there a reason? Are you afraid that you might get nigger-fied, by hanging around us?

Britt: How dare you talk to me like that. No, I am not afraid of you. Please, I just wanted to relax. I didn't feel like playing in the hot sun, and I won't respond to your last question.

Khari: I bet you know nothing about your people at all; for example: famous black writers, inventors, scientist, etc.. Can you name me at least three black authors?

Britt: Well, um, Alex Haley, and umm . You know I don't have to prove anything to you.

Khari: Just what I figured. You seem like one of those lost sisters who wants to be white. You can want all you want, but no matter how light you bleach your skin, have your nose re-arranged, wear fake hair and contact lenses, unless you were born white you will never be white. By the way, why are you wearing blue contact lenses? You are a pretty girl with out them. Be honest. How many black women, your color, do you know that have naturally blue eyes and blonde hair? (laughs) So what's your name Brit-ta-ny or something?

Britt: (she tries to act mad) By the way, it is, as a matter of fact, it is Brittany, and I enjoy wearing my lenses. They just give me a different look. Everyone thinks that I look exotic. Besides, blondes have more fun. What about your name Shack a Zulu? What kind of name is that? It sounds so ethnic.

Khari: It's Khari, and it means Kingly in Africa. Who ever sold you that bull-shit about exotic is sick. I shouldn't be having as much fun as I am, because I am not blonde. What's wrong? Please!!. You should get rid of all that mess and expose your true self.

Brittany: I know that I am gorgeous. I could care less what you think about my looks. You must find me intriguing, because you are over here.

Khari: No, I don't find you exotic or gorgeous. I find you mixed up, and I feel for my people who think that white is right just because it's white.

Brittany: Listen Khari, or Mr. King, if you came over here to bother me and humiliate me, I just want you to know that my boyfriend has a black belt.

Khari: Well, I know crazy. Girl, I didn't come over here to bother you. You are so mixed-up. You are the type of black that once you have made it, you want to disassociate yourself from your people. You probably think of me and my friend as low-lives. I feel sorry for people like you, because if you don't wake up soon, then you will have a bitter life. I am out of here.

Brittany: Ah, wait a minute, How dare you come over here and attack my character and the way I look. Then, you decide to walk away. You've got your nerve.

Khari: So, what is it Britt? I call a spade: a spade, or should I say a wannabe: a wannabe. You want me to attack your character and stay. I think that you kind of like me. All other men probably kiss your butt. I only kiss lips when a woman earns it.

Britt: (smiling). Well, I heard today, in church, that you majored in Engineering. That was my major at first then I changed it to Computer Science. What company will you be working for?

Khari: Oh, so now we are talking. Rockheed.

Britt: So, what are you reading?

Khari: It is a book about Malcolm X.

Britt: Is it about Zorro or something?

Khari: (cracking up laughing). No, it is about a black Muslim who discovers himself, as well as his black people and tries to speak the truth about the black man.

Britt: Didn't he teach about hating white people and said that they were the reason for all of our problems?

Khari: Well, that was his belief at first, but after returning from Mecca, he had a different view about white people. He wanted to tell all the other Muslims, as well as black people, that the white man wasn't the one who was the problem. We were the problem ourselves. It went against what the Muslims were teaching at the time, so he was assasinated. No one knows who really did it, but a lot of people believe the CIA bribed the Muslims to do it.

Britt: Very interesting.

Khari: Would you like to read it? You might learn a thing or two about yourself and your people. I have other books you can read to enlighten yourself.

Britt: I heard that all those books teach hatred towards white people.

Khari: You heard? Why not go to the source and read and

understand? These books teach that until we love ourselves we can't love anyone else. Rev. O.C. preaches it all the time. We have to stop blaming everyone else for our problems and heal ourselves. We can't afford to hate anyone, because we have to live in this world together, but you must take care of your own first.

Britt: Maybe I may glance through it. How do I get it back to you after I finish it?

Khari: Considered it a gift. If I can save one black person, then I have done my job. Well, you take care, and stay black my sister. I better get back over there to finish kicking your friend's butts(starts walking away).

Britt: Please don't hurt them!!!

Khari: I meant in volleyball. Wow, what kind of image do you have of us? You remind me of the white women who grab their purses whenever they see one of us, and you are black. Lord, help her!

Brittany: Hey Khari, (totally embarrassed, writes her number). Here is my number. Maybe you can call and give me the names of some of the other books I can read, and tell me where I might obtain them. Only use my number for that reason. Don't try calling me for anything else. I am engaged.

Khari: (takes number) Ms. Thang, I would never think about calling you for anything else. You are too confused. I admire and respect a strong black woman who is confidant with herself and who loves being black. You have no soul.

Britt: Wait a minute. You have put me down for the last time. Just because I refuse to walk around speaking ebonics, playing loud music, splitting verbs, and don't hate white people doesn't make me less of a black woman. Besides, what good is it for me to learn about black history?, when that happened years ago?

Khari: You have to know where you have been to know where you are going, my sista.

Britt: I am not finished. We need to stop reflecting on the past and concentrate on the future. We can't change the past no matter what we do. I am so tired of blacks always using the past for a reason for laziness, welfare, drug dealers, un-wed mothers, run-away fathers, and so on.. Blacks wrote the book on excuses for all their down-falls. So when I start seeing blacks getting educated and off of welfare, and being responsible for their children, then I will probably be proud of them.

Khari: First of all, I do agree that we should stop making excuses and should get more educated, but we need to be exposed first. A lot of our people only see one way of life. It is up to people like your friends and mine to go into the ghettos and expose our children to an alternative way of life. I am not saying live in the ghetto, but we do have an obligation to go back and help our people.

Britt: Well I have never lived in the ghetto, so I have no idea about the people there. Matter of fact, I have never seen a ghetto except on television. My parents made it a point to not expose me to the ghetto, because they didn't want me to feel guilty about how we lived. You blacks have a way of doing that to those of us who have succeeded in life. They felt that since we did not grow up in the ghetto, why concern ourselves about it. The whites don't.

Khari: So this started with your family. Boy, I really feel sorry for you, all of you. They are probably only one generation away from growing up in the ghetto. They definitely didn't always have what they do now. You know Brittany, I am really hurt and shocked about blacks like you. No one is saying that you shouldn't feel good about making it, or your life style. I am just saying don't forget where you came from once upon a time. You know, if anything ever went down in life which challenges you bougie blacks who think that they are no longer black, the first place they run is back to the black community. Then, they want to be black again. The whites are your friends while everything is going good, but just let you do or say something that goes against the grain of their life then you are just a niggah again. We have seen it recently with the trial. You know you always refer to blacks as "you all", like you are not black: like Spike Lee says, " Wake Up."

Britt: Well Khari, thanks for the Black Education 101 course. As I said, I will glance at your book. (putting the book in her bag) I'll be looking forward to your call. TTFN.

Khari: Yeah, Ta Ta for now to you too. Don't look surprised that I know what that means. You know Brittany, I didn't even scratch the surface, so don't thank me. Read the book and maybe you will want more knowledge about my people, since you don't consider yourself one of us,(laughs and walks away).

(Soon as Khari walks away, Britt pulls the book out and starts reading it. Khari turns around and sees her doing this, but she doesn't see him watching her. He smiles and says to himself, it's about time you wake up Ms. Van Winkle).

(Meanwhile, back at the volleyball game it's time for the final serve.

Eric: Hey, the ski club is getting ready to start the men and women's swim suit contest. You guys all want to walk over and check it out? (everyone says yeah).

(Eric and Kolby pair off, Landon and Om, Lance and Tanika and everyone else walks over together talking and laughing about the game. They proceed to watch the contest. After the contest it is becoming dusk).

Omunique: It is getting late. I have to get back and pick up the boys from my mom before they drive her crazy.

Landon: Boy, how fast did the time fly. I had one of the best times that I've had in my life with you and your friends. Your friend Eric can talk a lot of trash. Your cousin Khari, seems to be a really, real brother and very serious.

Omunique: Yeah, Eric is always the life of the party and Khari really cares about his people. He feels we have too much division among our own people. He is always trying to enlighten people about who they are.

Landon: Boy, I wish that he could enlighten Brittany. The rest of us are on our way. We were all confused until recently, but not Brittany. She doesn't want to have anything to do with anything or anyone that she considers stereotypical of our race.

Omunique: So is that the reason she didn't come over here? She thinks that we are stereotypical of our race? You don't have to answer. I know she does, I can see it in her eyes. She is probably the type that thinks that I am a single mother on welfare and just looking for a man to take care of me and my children.

Landon: Well you have hit the nail on the head. You are very observant. But don't be too hard on her. She is a product of her environment. Like we all were. All of our parents are what you might call the bougie blacks who have forgotten who they are and where they came from and who want nothing or no one to remind them of it.

Omunique: You know it's people like her that can give women like me an inferiority complex. No one has walked in my shoes, so they don't know why I chose to keep my children. Yes, I could have had an abortion, but I was at the point in my life where I felt that I had to be responsible for my irresponsibility. There comes a point in your life when you can't keep making mistakes and blaming everyone else. It is just like when you are traveling on the freeway, and you get off on the wrong exit: either you keep traveling farther away from your destination, or you turn around and go right back to the right exit and continue to your destination. Every woman who has a child out-of-wedlock is not on welfare. Some of us are working extremely hard to give our children a better life, as well as trying to better ourselves. No one said it would be easy.

Landon: Omunique you don't have to justify your reasons for choosing to keep your children. To be frankly honest, I chose the other way when Britt and I were faced with the situation. I was not ready to be a parent and neither was Britt. I look at each person as an individual. I don't see you as someone who is just trying to milk the system. You have gone on and graduated from college and will be embarking on a career which will support you and your children. I have only known you very shortly, but it doesn't take a mental colossal to see that you are a dynamite person.

Omunique: Why thank you Landon. You know most men don't see my attributes. All they see is me as a liability with two children. I find myself constantly trying to sell myself. It's like I am crying out for them to see what an asset I am. It's funny how our society is. A man can go out and make babies all over the world, but because he doesn't have the children with him he can start a new life all over. Where as, the woman is left with the children. She has to hope that someone will appreciate her and her children and marry her.

Landon: I understand what you are saying, and yes there is a double standard in society. I wish they would put more responsibility on these dead beat dads. My dad always told me to respect a woman, and if I did get a woman pregnant I would share the responsibility and support of that child. I would be around that child just as much as the mother is, regardless if we chose to marry or not. Omunique, I know it is a challenge to meet a good man for you as well as your children, but if a person really loves you, he should love your children just as much. It is like buying a stereo. You have to buy the speakers too. You can't have one without the other. Being the type of person you are, some one will come along. Who knows, you might be talking to that person?

Om: (blushing), I'm so sure. Oh, your parents and friends would disown you if you ever thought about marrying a woman with children. Why do you think they arranged your marriage to Britt, so this type of thing wouldn't happen? Heaven forbid.

Landon: That may be true, but I live my own life, and if my friends are true friends they would accept who I choose, and if not, to hell with them. Even though I hate saying this, the same goes with my parents. I choose who I want in my life. Remember when I told you things are not always what they seem between Britt and me? Well, I don't love her, and I don't think that she really loves me. I had a lot of thinking to do while I was away at college. Either I could go on and play the charade with Britt for the sake of my family, or I could become my own man and pick someone who I know will make me happy. I am the one who has to live with Britt, not them. I just haven't found the opportune time to tell everyone. I know there are going to be a lot of tears and disappointment. My mother and her mother are already planning on making this wedding the event of the Buppie community.

Omunique: Boy, Landon, I would hate to be in your shoes. Your life is almost like a fairy-tale. You know what it reminds me of, that Eddie Murphy movie "Coming to America." I thought these things only happen in the movies. I would love to stick around just to see how it turns out.

Landon: Hey, you know I never thought about it that way. (laughing) Well the way I feel right now, you may be the girl I came to America to get.

Omunique: Oh quit it. Like I say, you are a cajoler.

(Unbeknownst to both Landon and Om, Kolby has been listening to everything. She realizes that she really likes Omunique, and feels bad for Landon with the burden he will be facing with Britt and his parents).

Kolby: (walks up) Hey Landon, what's up?

Landon: (startled) Hey Kolby. I don't know if you had a chance to formally meet Omunique. (introduces them to each other).

Kolby: I have to be honest with you Landon, I overheard everything, and I just want you to know that I am behind you 100 percent with whatever decisions you make in life.

Omunique: Oh my gosh!! I thought that you and Brittany were best friends. Well, let me let you know that I am not trying to take her man. I respect relationships especially black ones. We already have a hard time trying to stay together.

Kolby: Please, you don't have to justify anything with me. I have been friends with Landon way before Brittany came into the picture; at least ten years. Landon is a very good man. I have always liked him, but I am just like a sister to him. He deserves a good woman like you. I will go and talk to your parents and anyone else you need to talk to, Landon, when it is time. You, know Omunique, we all woke up while we were away in school. We all realized that no matter what our social or economic status is, we are all still black. Ms. Britt realizes it also, but she doesn't want to accept it. Don't get me wrong, Britt is not a bad person, we were all just like her a while ago. Two years ago we probably would not be sitting here having this conversation with you, or playing volleyball with you and your friends. Britt just needs a reality check, and quick before it is too late.

Landon: I knew if anyone understood it would be you Kolby. Thanks for your support, but I have to do this myself. It is nice to know that I have a friend like you. You see Om, it is all right if I call you that isn't it? I heard your friends call you that?

Omunique: That's all right, Landon. So you are telling me you all just started realizing who you really are? It's a shame that we have let the media and everyone else make us feel bad about ourselves. I am not in the position to judge anyone. I am just glad that you all woke up, and I hope that others wake up. We can't do anything with ourselves until we open our eyes up to who we really are and love ourselves.

Kolby: Hey, Omunique, I heard in church today that you are going to be working for one of the major network news departments. How exciting. I can appreciate a single mother going after her career. I know it must be hard, but you keep Christ in your life and stay surrounded by good people. You are definitely pretty and personable enough to make it. I can see why Landon likes you. Your light from within is truly shining.

Omunique: Why thank you Kolby. I am looking forward to the challenge. I just always knew that I wanted a better lifestyle for me and my boys. I could have given up when the chips were against me, but my dad wouldn't let me. By the way, you're going to be working for a pretty nice company yourself.

Kolby: Yeah, I guess, but I eventually want to own my own black advertising company.

Landon: Well Kolby, I think we all better get going, Britt has sulked enough by herself. Let's round up everyone. They are still over there dancing.

Kolby: I will go and round everyone up, and Omunique, it was really nice meeting you. I am sure that I am going to see you again real soon(glares at Landon and smiles).

Omunique: Same here Kolby. I hope that you don't think that I am trying to come between you and your friend, or trying to take your friend's man.

Kolby: By no means at all. I was teasing Britt the other day when Landon was taking your children back to you, that she had some competition. Never did I imagine it would happen. He stayed gone too long. When he returned, I saw a spark in his eyes that I had never seen before. Besides, I never thought he and Britt belonged together. It's just that our parents feel they can control our lives, even down to whom we marry. Take care hon,bye-bye.

Landon: So Ms. Omunique can I call you tonight? I would love to continue our conversation, and make plans to see you away from the beach.

Omunique: Sure, but call me after 9:00. The children should be in bed by then.

(Everyone is saying bye and how much they enjoyed each other. They are all still partying while walking back to their spaces).

(Landon walks up to Brittany, she is so intensely into the book she doesn't even hear all the noise, or notice that everyone is returning).

Landon: Hey Britt, what do you have there? What are you reading?

Britt: (trying to hide the book). Oh it is nothing, it is just a book about wedding plans. What is all the ruckus? you guys are acting like a bunch of low-life niggahs. You go and play a game of volleyball with them and come back acting like them. You get close to dirt, and the next thing you know you get dust in your eyes.

(Everyone looks surprised and angered. Someone says, "shut up you oreo.")

Kolby: Let me handle this you guys. You know Britt, I am just about tired of your black remarks like you are not. First of all, they were the nicest people you could meet. We didn't have to act like someone who we're not. They accepted us as we were. Why is it we are considered niggahs when we want to party and get loud? Oh, I know why, because it is not socially accepted for people who are black to party, but let a white person do it and it is considered that they are just having fun. Look over there at that group of whites. They are all drunk and loud and boisterous. We have not even had a drink. So you tell, me Missy, what's the difference? (Everyone says yeah. In the background a group of whites are partying, downing beer and are really loud).

Britt: What the hell is wrong with you? How dare you talk to me like that? One day of hanging out with the so-called homeys and you come back thinking that you are one of them. Yes it is different when whites party than when niggahs party.

Lance: Well what is the difference Britt? You don't see us picking up trash cans and tossing them, or screaming, or throwing each other around, and using vulgar language. For my own edification, please tell me who are the rowdy ones?

Britt: I don't have to answer yours or anyone else's questions. I am ready to go Landon, right now! I don't know any of you. A couple of hours have turned you all into savages.

Lance: Just as I thought Whenever you can't answer something you always say I don't have to answer. You know Landon you might as well have had a white girl, because she sure isn't black. (everyone laughs).

Britt: Landon are you going to stand there and let him talk to me like that?

Landon: Why no, I am going to start walking to the car. (everyone laughs).

Britt: I don't believe you are embarrassing me in front of everyone. Wait until I talk to your mother. Take me home this very minute, and another thing Kolby, don't bother to call me tomorrow morning.

Kolby: Okay. If that is what you want Britt.

(Landon and Brittany head for the car. While they are walking, she is scolding him for humiliating her in front of their friends. He is too busy thinking about Om, so he has tuned her out. They make the ride home in total silence. They arrive at Britts house. She immediately gets out of the car and slams the door).

Scene 8

Landon is at home. He has just finished taking a shower while Om has just said her prayers with the boys and put them down to sleep. She then goes and takes a shower. Landon and Om are both constantly looking at the clock. It's 9:00 p.m).

Landon: (on phone) Hello, may I speak to Omunique please?

Omunique: This is she.

Landon: Well, this is your tall, dark, handsome prince charming, who is going to make your life a little easier to live. I can't say I can take you away from all your worries, but maybe I can alleviate a few of them. Have you put the children to sleep yet?

Omunique: Allright now, I told you your name was going to be Mr. Cajoler. Yes, I did, The little tikes are sound asleep.

Landon: I am glad that you decided to give me your number. I know that you were very hesitant at first.

Omunique: Yeah, I still am. As I told you, I don't believe in talking to an engaged or married man. I am not into games, and I don't want someone to hang around because they think that I am needy or something. We, meaning the black woman, already have enough to deal with everyday. For example, our men going to other races of women, or them taking our men, bi-sexual, gay, or them being in prison. I would never want to take another black man from my black sister deliberately. You black men are a hot commodity. I heard what you said today, however, I still have a lot of trepidation about talking to you.

Landon: First of all Omunique, I am not a toy which you just take away from someone. I make my own choices as of lately, and I choose to get to know you better. I am not saying that I am going to jump into a relationship with you. I do believe in the cliché that we should be friends first, then lovers. Meeting you has just reconfirmed the decision I had already made about me and Britt. So I would never try to use or abuse you. You are too good for that. I just want to get to know you better, to see if there is a possibility of us getting closer. I know what I am feeling is real.

Omunique: We do agree on being friends first, but I think you need to close one book before you open another one. In the interim, I am willing to be your friend. This is the first time in my life I went against my principle about engaged men. There is just something I feel that is very honest and sincere about you.

Landon: Well, I thank you for going against your principles. So how about me picking you up for dinner tomorrow? Your choice.

Omunique: Okay, that sounds good. I need to call my baby-sitter. She is this wonderful woman named Diane who is always there for me and the boys. I found her through an ad I ran in our local paper. God really blessed me to bring her into our lives.

Landon: It is nice to know you have someone who you can trust with your children. By the way, I will pay for the baby-sitter. I think any man who takes a woman out should do so. The time he is spending with that woman is keeping her away from that child.

Omunique: Oh, I would never. I can handle it. Besides, they're my children not yours.

Landon: Then either you bring the children, or let me pay the baby-sitter.

Omunique: Okay, you win. Only one other man has done that for me in my life. Most men feel it is the woman's responsibility.

Landon: Then you haven't been around a real man. So where do you want to go and eat?

Omunique: How about the Cafe Avenue? It is a real nice soul food restaurant close to Baldwin Hills. Hey, don't you live in the area? You should know the restaurant.

Landon: Sorry, I don't. Is it like Henry's.

Omunique: Henry's doesn't serve real soul food. That is avant-garde soul food. There is a difference between real soul food and avant-garde soul food. Real soul food sticks to your ribs.

Landon: Well my parents have never exposed my sister and I to real soul food. They said that is why so many of us die quickly. They also contribute the food to our people being overweight I told you they wanted to lose anything that was stereotypical of our race.

Omunique: Well, anything done excessively will kill you, but real soul-food is great to eat every once in a while, and I sure do have a taste for some smothered pork-chops, greens, candy yams, and hot water cornbread.

Landon: Okay, what the heck? I guess it is a part of my culture.

I can see we are going to be great for each other. You will expose me to some new things and I will expose you to some new things. What time shall I call on you for dinner tomorrow?

Omunique: Well you can call on me about 6:30, and that way I should be back home by no later than 9:30, 10:00 at the latest.

Landon: I do need directions. What part of the city do you live in?

Omunique: Have you ever heard of Carson?

Landon: Yes, I have heard of it. Isn't it near Compton?

Omunique: Not far, but you don't have to be afraid. Quiet as it is kept, Compton has some really good parts in it. The media paints a bad picture of the city. My neighborhood is very nice. The neighbors are all retired or young professional couples.

Landon: Well thanks for making me feel safe. I don't believe I have ever been in that part of town. Give me the directions

(Omunique gives him the directions).

Landon: My sister, I think that you are going to help me see the light much better about myself and my people.

Omunique: First of all, you have to get it right my brotha; it is "my sista",(they both laugh). Well, my brotha I will see you tomorrow. I am exhausted, I better get some rest. It was nice talking to you.

Landon: Okay my sista. The pleasure was mine. I will call you tomorrow and reconfirm our date. I have a car phone if I get lost. Good night Oh, and say hello to Jordan and Randolph for me. (they hang up the phone).

Scene 9
Khari: (dialing Britt's number). Hello. May I speak to Brit-

tany please?

Britt: (very mean) Who's calling?

Khari: This is your knight in shiny black armor coming to carry you off on his black shiny stallion.

Britt: (blushing and smiling from ear to ear). Oh, this must be the guy who attacked my character at the beach. Are you calling to chew me out some more? You know, I think that I had enough abuse today. You know that I am looking for my Knight in shiny white armor, to come and carry me off on his white horse.(They both laugh).

Khari: Well, I said that to illicit a laugh, but you know me, there is some truth in it. This is Khari.

Britt: Oh yeah. I couldn't quite remember your name. It is kind of different. I thought I told you to call me only about the book. I haven't even read it yet(lying she has just about finished the book). You want it back now?

Khari: You probably have finished it. I must confess I saw how into the book you were at the beach. I turned and saw you take it out of your bag when I walked away. You act like you are embarrassed about it. I know that a little glimmer of light is coming on, because you are being a whole lot nicer to me.

Britt: Well, it is pretty interesting reading. I wouldn't mind reading some more books. Not to say that I am going to change my opinion about anything. You probably have never read any other books but black books.

Khari: See, there you go stereotyping again. Just because I didn't go to an Ivy League school doesn't mean I am not into the classics. I read all types of author's books such as, Hawthorne Dickens, Carroll, Hemingway, James Baldwin, California Cooper, B.B. Moore Campbell and Toni Morrison just to name a few. You get the picture?

Britt: I knew them all until you got to the last four. Who are they. I am very impressed. You seem well versed.

Khari: It figures. I threw them in purposefully. They are black authors. Unlike you, I read all types of works. I just called you to give you a list of some other good books to read. (names them for her).

Britt: Why thank you. When I find the time, I will browse through them.

Khari: Yeah, right. Just like you browsed through Malcom X. Well, I will throw your number away and won't ever bother you again. I just hope that I was responsible for helping someone find herself and loving herself just the way she is. Later, my Nubian Princess. I usually say stay black, but with you I need to say get black(laughs).

Britt: Funny. Ah, wait a minute Khari To be frankly honest, I have been reading your book and I am practically finished. I am finding it very fascinating. I am eager to read more. I know sometimes I can be a little crass and act nonchalant.

Khari: To say the least.

Britt: Well, I don't really know where to purchase these types of books. Maybe(phone beeps) could you please hold?

Khari: (smiling) Sure. (he knows that she kind of likes him now).

Landon: Hey Britt. I hope that you are feeling much better now.

Britt: How can I help you?

Landon: Listen Britt, you don't have to be so cold. I know that you are on the other line, so I will make it quick. I can't see you tomorrow evening. I have something I need to do.

Britt: Fine, I was just about to call you and tell you the same thing. Well, I do have another call. Bye. (she clicks off before he can say good bye).

Landon: Boy, she really must be pissed. She usually gives me a hard time about breaking a date. (wipes the sweat from his brow).

Britt: Ah, um Khari thanks for holding. Getting back to what I was saying, why don't we get together tomorrow around 4:00 and you can take me to the book store where I can buy this list of books which you have given me. Um, we may be able to get a bite to eat while we are out. Just to let you know before you get the big head. This is not a date.

Khari: First of all, you didn't bother to ask me if I had other plans. You just assumed I didn't. Well you may push your man and friends around, but that doesn't work in my world. If you want me to respect you, then you must first respect me and yourself. Hold on, let me check my Franklin. (never leaves the phone).

Britt: (not knowing that Khari is still on the phone). I hope that he can go. Everyone says I am pushy, and never considers anyone else's time. Why did I understand it, when he said it. um.

Khari: (feeling sorry for her, starts turning pages) Well Ms. Britt you are out of luck.

Britt: Well, I have to go.

Khari: Wait. Don't assume the worst! You are out of luck, because no one else has booked me up for tomorrow, so you are stuck with me.

Britt: Great. Where can I meet you?
Khari: Oh, it is like that. Wouldn't want me coming up to your door to meet your parents. Where I come from, we always

pick up the lady at her door and never blow the horn. We respect her household as well as her parents. You would probably pass me off as the gardener or something. Well, whatever. It's funny, just a minute ago when you thought that I couldn't make it you were ready to get off the phone, because you were not getting your way.

Britt: Well, first of all Khari, I did say that this wasn't a date. Besides, why should I continue to talk to you if you couldn't make it. I thought that our conversation was finished. The fact about you not coming to my house has nothing to do with you. I just don't like my parents knowing my business. After all, I am an engaged woman.

Khari: No problem, Brittany. Spare me the excuses. Where do you live? I mean what part of the city do you live in so that I can arrange a meeting spot?

Britt: I live in Ladera Hts.

Khari: That figures. You live right in the hood where all the black book stores and black shops are. Probably passed them a million times.

Britt: Well, just give me the address of the place and I will meet you there at 4:00.

Khari: Cool.(gives her the address). Call me if for any reason you can't make it. My number is 555-2323.

Britt: Thanks. By the way, I apologize for assuming you had no life before me(laughs).

Khari: No, apologies necessary, by the time I finish enlightening you, you will see that you have been living an imitation of life. It would be nice to see what is really behind those contact lenses, and under the blonde wig. I may be pleasantly surprised. Not! Sweet dreams my Nubian princess.

Britt: (blushes) Who knows. Wishes sometimes do come true.

Good night Khari. (picks book up immediately).

Scene 10

(Kolby stops by Britt's house it is around 2:30 p.m. Britt is getting dressed and prancing in the mirror. She likes what she sees).

Kolby: Britt, I just want to apologize for yesterday. I was pretty mean, but it upsets me when you talk about our people the way you do. I just wish that you could see what we all see now about ourselves, our parents, our people. That's all.

Britt: Well, maybe I did deserve some of that.

Kolby: Girl, let me feel your head. Are you sick or something? You have never admitted to being wrong about anything. What is really going on? You and Landon make up? You look excited. I was going to stop by his house next. So where are you two going?

Britt: Kolby, don't go by there. I must swear you to secrecy. I am not going out with Landon. I have a date with someone else. How do I look?

Kolby: No, who is it? You sure you are not sick? You look great!! No wig or contact lenses. Please don't keep me in suspense. Who is it? Whomever it is, you really like him. I have never ever seen this look about you before. I am with you 24/7. When was it possible for you to meet someone? I didn't realize you had all this natural beauty. I can't believe this is your hair. It is beautiful. What is really going on?

Britt: Calm down. One question at a time. First of all, you really think so? I kinda like it myself. I will kill you if you let this out. I probably shouldn't open my mouth. You seem to have gotten diarrhea at the mouth lately. You have to swear.

Kolby: About yesterday, I was making a point. I have never

divulged anything about you in all the years we have been friends, and I know a lot.

Britt: Well, you do have a point there. Okay, well, it is not really a date I am meeting someone at Eshwan bookstore.

Kolby: You are serious. How did you find out about this place. It is a black book store. You would never be caught in a place like that. I know you are telling the truth; just the fact that you know the name of the store.

Britt: Well, you see, the other day when we were at the beach, one of the boys from the hood.

Kolby: Britt please. There you go again.

Britt: Allright. Remember the guy at church who is going to be an Engineer?

Kolby: The tall, fair-skinned, good looking brother?

Britt: Well, I wouldn't say he is all that (blushing). You think he is handsome?

Kolby: Why yes I do. But not as handsome as his friend Eric, who I talked to a little bit yesterday.

Britt: Well, getting back to the point, he came over while I was sitting alone, after refusing to join you guys in volleyball. He proceeded to give me a black history course 101, and well, he left this book for me to read(Shows her book). He told me there were other books I should read, so I gave him my number; just to tell me more about the books of course.

Kolby: (very surprised) Of course.

Britt: Well he called me last night and one thing led to another, and I agreed to meet him at the book store and then we may get a bite to eat.

Kolby: I couldn't see you letting him come to the house so that Dominique and Michael could meet him.

Britt: It is not a date.

Kolby: Well, well, well, Ms Uptown girl herself trying to get culturalized. I am all for it. I will keep my mouth shut if you promise to do one thing for me.

Britt: What is that Ms. Blackmailer?

Kolby: Tell him that I would like for his friend, Eric, to call me. You can give him my number.

Britt: You are not serious are you Kolby? After today I don't plan on seeing him again. Think of what my parents and Landon would think of me if they knew.

Kolby: First of all, I am very serious and secondly, I don't think Landon would care as much as you think he would. And forget your parents. You are the one who has to be happy in your life. You know, for a minute there, I thought that there was some hope for you. By the way, you look very good without those contact lenses and blonde wig, I must say again. No one would ever know you if they saw you.

Britt: What do you mean Landon wouldn't care? What do you know that I don't? You tell me now Kolby, or else.

Kolby: Or else what? There you go again with your kiddish threats. They don't work on me anymore, Britt. Anyway, about Landon, I was just talking off my head. I know he would be very upset if he knew (rolls her eyes).

Britt: All right Kolby. I will give Khari your number to give to Eric, but don't expect me to hang around you all.

Kolby: Why never Ms. Brittany.

Brittany: Well, I am out of here. I told him I would meet him at 4:00. I have a few runs I need to make. Of course I am not going to be on time. You know it is good to make them wait.

Kolby: Try cutting the games, and meet him on time. A man

like him doesn't have time for games.

Britt: We will see.

Scene 11

(At Khari's apt. Eric drops by: Khari is getting dressed).

Eric: Hey man let's go play some B-Ball.

Khari: (Putting on shoes) Can't, I have to meet someone at 4:00 at Eshwan Bookstore.

Eric: Don't tell me you have found another Rip Van Winkle? This one must be a lady, because you look rather sharp my brotha, and you are putting on Cool water. Who is it man?

Khari: You wouldn't believe me if I told you.

Eric: Try me

Khari: Remember the sister at church, who graduated from Yale and majored in Computer Science?

Eric: Yeah, the stuck up broad who thinks she is white. Black as she is wearing blue contact lenses and a blonde wig.

Khari: First of all Eric, no black woman is a broad, and yes, she is stuck up with shit that needs to be drained from her, and I think there is hope.

Eric: You are right. We shouldn't degrade our sisters. I am sorry man, but go on. You must admit she has been seriously white-washed by the media and society.

Khari: Yes, I do admit to that fact, however, who are we to really judge. We don't know how she became confused. I feel for all my people who are embarrassed by who and what they are. You really have to be strong to function in our society. Well, anyway, I am meeting her to inform her of what black books to read so that she can understand herself better as well as her people. Then maybe she can learn to love herself the way she is.

Eric: Oh, yeah, what about her fiancee?

Khari: I don't know and I don't care. This is not a date. She probably won't see me again after this. She seems just like a user getting what she wants and then dropping you like a hot potato, especially if you don't meet her qualifications.

Eric: I think that this is far more than an educational class. I know you are intrigued by her, you don't have to say it. I see it all on your face (starts singing, "Ain't it funny about the way you feel shows all over your face" laughs). Just don't get hurt man.

Khari: As I told you before, I think the sister is ready to come up from the dark, or should I say from the white. I am pointing her in the right direction.

Eric: Well how do you think Om would feel if she knew her cousin was meeting the woman who tried to dis her?

Khari: This needs to go no farther than my place. Word?

Eric: Word. But there is one thing you can do for me. See if you can get her friend Kolby's number for me. I think she was giving me some rhythm yesterday at the beach. We talked briefly and seemed to click pretty well. I wanted to ask her for her number, but I thought that she would've dissed me. You know, cause she is one of those bougie girls. She kept smiling at me.

Khari: Man, she was laughing at you, trying to figure out what you were (both laugh). I will see what I can do, but next time don't you have fear of anything or anyone. You are just as good as anyone on this earth, but you must believe it. How a man thinks becomes his reality.

Eric: You are right again man, I hear you. I know that I am just as good as she is, despite the fact that she has money.

Khari: Well, there you go and don't you ever forget it. It is 3:00 I better get going. You know how I am a stickler for time. I bet she is going to be late just because. I know her type.

Eric: Call me later man. Let me know how it went. If you wake up someone like her, then I know you are the chosen one(laughs). Stay black, and don't forget about Kolby's number.

Khari: I am a 100 percenter (shakes hands). I will not forget the digits.

Scene 12

(Brittany arrives at the bookstore 10 minutes to 4:00 in her new red convertible BMW with the top down. She sits in the parking lot still looking in the mirror at herself).

(Khari drives up in his in new black Toyota Camary. They spot each other and smile. Khari parks next to Britt. He doesn't realize who she is. He is really checking her out, and smiles and says hi).

Britt: Hello how are you?(She realizes he doesn't know who she is).

Khari: Very well. You know you have probably heard this line a million times, but I just want you to know how beautiful you are. You are a black beauty. It is rare these days to find a sister without anything fake on them.

Britt(blushing) Oh really, well I thank you for the compliment. Are you meeting anyone special here today.

Khari: By the way, I am. A friend of mine who is confused about her blackness. If only she could see you. I think that she would appreciate herself. I have a feeling she might be just as beautiful as you are without the fake lenses and hair.

Britt: Khari, well you may have a point there. I love the way I look, and I can't believe it took me this long to see.

Khari: Brittany Oh my gosh, Girl, you are the bomb. You have been hiding all this beauty all this time. My sista, My sista. There is a God up there. That is a nice car Brittany, was it a graduation present?

Britt: Why matter fact, yes My parents chose it for me. It was waiting for me when I got home from school. Yours is not bad either, I used to drive a Camary in high school.

Khari: Well you certainly have moved up. Must be nice to have parents who can afford to buy you a new car. I had to buy mine by myself. I make the notes every month.

Britt: Well it does help out having parents who can afford to buy you a car. You know I have passed this place a million times, but never noticed it.

Khari: Just what I said last night(under his breath).

Britt: What did you say?

Khari: Oh, just thinking out loud Well come on, let's get this over with.

(They walk into the store browsing thru books, laughing and having a good time. Khari picks up a book).

Khari: Brittany, if there is no other book you buy, please buy this one. (HOW TO KILL YOUR WILLIE LYNCH?)

Britt: What is it about.

Khari: This one you have to read for yourself, and then figure it out.

Britt: Well since you highly recommend it, I will make sure it is the first one I read. (Britt pays for her other books purchase with her gold American Express card. Khari pulls out the

"HOW TO KILL YOUR WILLIE LYNCH?" book and pays for it).

Khari: Consider this a personal gift from me to you.

Britt: Why thank you, Khari. Hey Khari, lets go and get something to eat. Excuse me, I mean if you have the time would you like to go get something to eat?

Khari: You know, Brittany you may be all right. After all, you can learn. Why don't we go over to the Cafe Avenue. It's right down the street from here. It is a good Soul food restaurant. It's a quarter to 5, we should get there right before the dinner crowd.

Britt: Okay, is it similar to Henrys?

Khari: Girl, that isn't real soul-food. They have watered it down for the white folks. I am talking about real soul food.

Britt: Well all right. I have never eaten real soul food. Since I am in the mode of exploring today, why not? May I suggest that we leave your car here and take mine? I would just hate for something to happen to it.

khari: I was going to suggest that.

Britt: Boy, I thought that you were going to give me the line about your car is just as valuable as mine, which it is, however, I think that someone would go for my car first, than yours.

Khari: No need to justify Brittany. I feel the same way too. See I am not all that bad. (they both laugh).

(They get into her BMW and Brittany flies down the street with the top down blasting the music and laughing at Khari's jokes. They arrive at the restaurant with Khari giving directions,and Brittany purposely does the opposite being humorous. Khari gets out and opens Brittany's door. They walk into the restaurant.They sit down and look at the menu).

Britt: I don't know what is good why don't you order for us?

Khari: (to waitress) We will take two orders of smothered porkchops, cabbage, yams, rice and macaroni and cheese.

Britt: You know my mother never had Andre prepare this type of food. She said it was too fattening, and was a number one killer amongst blacks. Our chef basically served all different types of dishes, but never soul food.

Khari: You grew up with a chef? I only thought that the Fresh Prince lived liked that (they both laugh).

Britt: So tell me a little about yourself. How did you end up majoring in Engineering?

Khari: Well, my cousin Omunique and I...

Britt: (very surprised) Is that your cousin?

Khair: My first cousin.

Britt: OOPS.

Khari: Yes, I heard how you tried to belittle her. She is a very intelligent, strong black woman. She is the most spiritual kind-hearted, humorous person you could ever meet. She is also a damn good mother.

Britt: Is she married?

Khari: No, and what difference does it make? It doesn't take away from the kind of woman she is. Never pre-judge another person until you have walked in their shoes. Her children's daddy was a jerk. He had two babies by her, but he drove her to leave him. He constantly put her down, and even had the nerve to tell her when she was pregnant with the second child that he hoped that she would lose the baby, because the infant mortality rate is high in black women.

Britt: Was he white?

Khari: No, but he is a high class corporate attorney who got off by putting her down to camouflage his own insecurities. He ended up getting another woman of another race pregnant and married her. This woman doesn't have half the attributes my cousin has, from what we have been told. She is so envious of my cousin and her children. He still treats Omunique like shit. He took two years of tearing her self-esteem down, or should I say she let him do it. It has now been four years since she left him, and her self-esteem is still not up to par like it used to be. Enough of my cousin's business. I just wanted to give you a little insight on her. So next time, just because you see a single woman with children doesn't mean she is always on welfare. My cousin has her BA in journalism, and she is going to be a very good reporter.

Britt: Well, her story does put a little twist on things. I guess there are always exceptions to the rule. So getting back to you.

Khari: Like I was saying, we're the first ones in our family who have graduated from college. We both finished Valedictorian We both also worked and put ourselves through school. I chose engineering because I am very good with numbers and I like the field. I did a couple of internships with several companies over the years, and you?

Britt: Well, I am a third generation of college graduates in my family on my father's side and a second on my mother's side. My mother is an attorney and my dad is a doctor. I have always been fascinated with numbers also. I first majored in Engineering, but as time went on I got into computers and loved it, so I changed my major to computer science. My parents always wanted the best for me in everything. They even arranged my marriage to Landon because in the social club my parents are in, Landon was considered the cream of the crop.

Khari: The more I hear about you the more amazed I am with

you. Your life is like a few of the positive black shows which I have seen on TV. Your parents sound like the Huxtables. The only difference is they loved being black. It's funny that you say how your family tries to ignore anything that would connect them with their roots, but arranged marriages were done by our ancestors in Africa. They were the ones who first started that, not the white man. Usually a women's marriage would be arranged. The higher the status her parents were, the better husband she would get. However, he had to prove himself worthy by competing in tribal rituals which tested his manhood. So, it's like I said before, you must know where you came from to know where you are going. I bet they don't know this info. By the way, how do you feel about Landon? Do you love each other?

Britt: I love him as a person, but I am not in love with him. Besides, what does love have to do with it. According to our parents, we will look great on paper: a corporate attorney and computer programmer for a Fortune 500 company. Why our salaries together will afford us all the material things we want in life. As far as his feelings, they're probably the same as mine. But like me, he won't go against his parents. I have more spine than he does.

Khari: That is absurd. You are about to marry a man who you don't love just because your parents say so, and because you think that material things will buy you happiness. What is happening to us? Whatever happened to the spontaneity of just falling in love. This is one of the reasons we are becoming insensitive and cruel to each other. Love has a lot to do with it. Tina Turner just didn't have real love in her life. How could she know what love is when she had the kind of life she had for years. She has become desensitized to love like so many of us have. A better song is by my man Stevie Wonder, "Love Is In Need of Love Today". While we are on the subject, if you get up early during the week, around 5:00 a.m., listen to 102.3 KJLH. Steve owns the station. A program comes on in the morning called Front Page. It deals with all types of issues about blacks.

Khari: Well, here is the food; smells absolutely wonderful. Wait until you taste it. Let's bless the food first(says a prayer).

Britt: (Amen). I am an early riser, so maybe one day I will check it out. I didn't know Stevie Wonder had his own radio station. This food is absolutely delicious. How could something so good be so bad for you?

Khari: Anything done in excess is bad for you. Don't get too attached to it. It can quickly ruin that beautiful shape of yours.

Britt: Yes sir, Mr. Khari.

Khari: I don't want to keep you out any longer, and besides this isn't a date, So eat up and lets get going.

Britt: (stuffing her face) Okay Khari. Maybe next time we can get started a little earlier and do something really fun.

Khari: Excuse me, who said anything about next time? I am not about to hang around a woman who is about to get married. I am not going to dis my black brother. There are enough women to go around, so I don't have to spend my time with an engaged woman. I am not a puppet that you can keep around for your amusement.

Britt: Aw, come on Khari. Didn't you have fun with me? We both have a lot in common. We seem to enjoy each other's company and besides, I need you to help me understand all these books I bought.

Khari: You know you could go up to USC or UCLA and take a black history course and they will help you understand much better than I. I am not a teacher. I just point people like you in the right direction, and then the rest is up to them.

Britt: Listen Khari, I have not had this much fun in my life in such a long time. I know that I am in an unusual situation with my relationship with Landon, but you have peaked my curiosity. I want to get to know you better.

Khari: They say "curiosity killed the cat".

Britt: And satisfaction brings it back.

Khari: You are too much. If you would just let yourself go and be your own person. I think that a real fantastic person could emerge from her cocoon. You know you could possibly fall in love with me, then what would you do?

Britt: Please don't say things like that. I am engaged to be married to Landon. You know the deal, so don't fall in love with me, and I won't with you.

Khari: Why? Would it be too hard of a pill for your parents and friends to swallow? I am not going to sweat you, because I already know the answer. Come on let's go. I have some work I need to do tonight.

Britt: (Hands Khari her gold American Express card). Here is the contribution for my half.

Khari: Keep your card. I have money to pay for us both, and you don't owe me a thing. I am the man, and yes I am still old-fashioned when it comes to certain things.

Britt:(SHOCKED) Why thank you.

Meanwhile:

Omunique: (is giving the children a briefing on how to treat the baby-sitter. She gives the baby-sitter her instructions). The children's meal is already prepared Don't feed them any later than 7:00. (The door bell rings. She rushes out and kisses the boys goodbye).

Omunique: Hi, Landon. I guess you didn't have any trouble finding it, you didn't call me.

Landon: It was a piece of cake; you gave very good directions. Boy, this is a nice neighborhood. Your house is nice also. I am impressed.

Omunique: Why thank you. I like it.

Landon: I have always wanted a woman who could be on time. Britt is always an hour or more late no matter what we do. I have even tried giving her an incorrect time so that we could make it to things on time, no luck.

Omunique: Please don't make this a night of comparisons.

Landon: Omunique, I'm sorry You are right, but you are like a breath of fresh air. Before we take off, let me get something for you to take into the house. (comes back with a bouquet of flowers two small trucks for the boys, and a magazine for Diane).

Omunique: Wow! How beautiful. You didn't have to. Now who is the magazine for?

Landon: Diane. I know my baby-sitter used to love to read when my sister and I went to sleep. I know that I didn't have to, but I wanted to. All mothers deserve something nice sometime, and so do your boys, and especially the baby-sitter.

Omunique: (tears in her eyes). Thank you very much (runs back in and gives the flowers to the baby-sitter to put in water and tells her where the vase is. She also gives the boys their trucks. they jump up and down with excitement).

Omunique: Diane, he bought this magazine for you.

Diane: Well, this is one of my favorite magazines. I started to get it today, but I ran out of money at the store. You sure he isn't a mind reader?

Omunique: That's what I was thinking.

Diane: I like him already. He seems to be a very considerate man. Good sign, as long as he doesn't over do it.

Omunique: I hear you. I kind of like him too(smiles and winks her eye).

Landon: (opens the door to his new black 500 SEL). Get in, my princess.

Omunique: Wow, my dream car. This is beautiful. It will be forever before I could even think about buying something like this.

Landon: It was my graduation present from my parents and grandparents.

Omunique: Why the four doors for a single man.

Landon: They anticipated Britt and I starting a family right-away.

Omunique: (sarcastically) um.

Landon: My parents believe that I should look the part now as a Corporate Lawyer. I told them I haven't passed the bar yet.

Omunique: You will, and you will do well.

Landon: What confidence you have in me. I like that. (they proceed to the restaurant. They are looking for a parking space when Landon spies a brand new, red BMW). Hey that looks like Britt's car, but no way would she be in a place like this.

Omunique: Just spiffy. You have the Benz and she has the Beamer, must be nice. So where is the house going to be in Bel Air?

Landon: I don't see a house for Britt and me.

Omunique: Well I was just going to say don't forget us po-folks down here.

Landon: I could never forget someone like you, and I don't

plan on it (stares at her very passionately). They can't find a parking place, so they go around the corner and come back. When they return the spot where the red Beamer was is open, so they park in it. They proceed to go into the restaurant.

Omunique: I will order for both of us, I think that the smothered steak with rice, greens and candied yams should be good.

Landon: Sounds good to me.

Landon: I hope that I am not prying, and I know you touched on it at the beach, but what actually happened with you and the boy's father? If it's personal, I understand.

Omunique: Well, we met at a fund raiser. He pursued me for about a month, until I finally gave in. He was an attorney just getting started in his career. I was just entering college. He always put me down because I was only getting an under graduate degree in Journalism. I got pregnant around 4 months after dating him. He abandoned me when I told him about the pregnancy. I thought about having an abortion, but a voice in my dreams told me to keep the child, and that every thing would be allright. I had the baby and after three months he begged me to come back to him. Everyone protested but I went back to him. Afterwards, I became pregnant again. I was 2 months pregnant when I left him again. He was verbally abusive to me. At one time he started getting physically abusive too. His parents gave me just as much hell. They wanted him to marry another attorney, or doctor. It got so bad that he and his parents insisted that I call him counselor because he was an attorney. When I left him, he told me "You know the infant mortality rate is high in black women. I hope you lose the baby." The irony of the whole story is he married a woman of another race without any education. I gave him the power to take away all my self-esteem, but now I am almost back to my old self, and I hope that I don't ever fall to that level again.

Landon: Boy, I am sorry to hear that. It bothers me that our black men will down a black woman, but give another woman of a different race a chance for the finer things in life. They are not man enough to deal with their own masculinity, they need someone who they can control and dominate. That is not love, that is slavery. His parents should have never been in your business anyway. Sounds like they controlled his life. Any man who has to put a woman down or anybody down to make himself look better, is very weak. He probably was the type to blame everyone else for his failures.

Omunique: You hit the nail on the head. Let's not talk anymore about this subject. I am still healing.

Landon: Okay, I can respect that. So what made you choose journalism?

Omunique: Because I have a gift to gab(laughs). I love people, and I am always curious to find out about people, places and things. Some people call it being noisy.

Landon: As I said before, you are going to make a wonderful reporter.

Omunique: I hope to. Now my turn. Why did you choose law? Oh, here is the food. Will you bless the food?

Landon: Uh, oh yeah, sure. (says something really quickly both say Amen). You know my grandfather and my dad are both attorneys, so I couldn't break the family tradition. Well I could have, but I love law, so I did it more for myself. I am just happy I did like the field, or it would had been difficult explaining why I didn't choose law.

Omunique: Well, my cousin Khari and I are the first college graduates in our family.

Landon: Well, I admire you. You finished up despite the odds against you doing it with two children. Says a lot about your character. That's it! Your ex was intimidated by your strength.

Hey this food is delicious. I like it.

Omunique: I figured you would.

Scene 13

(Britt and Khari arrive back at his car. There is an uncomfortable silence).

Britt: Well thank you, Khari, for everything. I really did enjoy myself. I do wish things were different.

Khari: Spare me the verbiage. You just read and listen to the station I told you to, and maybe after you awake from your imitation world, you may marry a down to earth brother, who you really love. You will see that all the superficial things don't mean a thing if you don't have someone who loves you and vice-versa. You take care, Brittany, and instead of saying stay black, I am again going to say get black..

Britt: Question. Why haven't you called me Britt?

Khari: Because I figured if your mother wanted you to be called Britt, she would had named you Britt. A lot is said about a person's name. It should be lived up to. It is your title. Besides it is too close to a word that would fit your character. I might slip. The only person I don't call by her full name is my cousin. She prefers Om and when we were children it was easier to say than her whole name. Anyone who meets her knows she is Unique.

Britt: Interesting. (she grabs his face, while he is trying to get out the door). She kisses him passionately for a long while.

Khari: Girl you are trying to mess with my head.

Britt: Can I possibly see you again?

Khari: You have my number. When you are ready to be real, and you have awakened from your snow white sleep, call me.

(he grabs her head and hand and kisses them).

Britt: (sits in her car and waits for Khari to get into his car. They wave goodbye to each other. She is crying and shaking her head, and thinking boy, I really like him, but what would my parents say? Oh please God help me to be strong, I think that he is the one for me).

Khari: (driving home). Man, I really like that girl. She does something to me. If you are listening God, please wake her up.

Scene 14

Landon: (arriving back at Om's house). Would it be wrong if I asked you for a kiss on the first date?

Omunique: We are both grown, and I don't believe in that first date rule all the time, so the answer to the question is no. (They kiss long and hard for a while. They both gasp and say wow to each other. It was one of those kisses that lets you know this is the one. There is an uncomfortable silence afterwards).

Landon: Well, let me walk you to the door. I had one of the best times I've had in my life. Oh Om, could you please give this to Diane?

Omunique: Really, I can't take this. Anyway she was only here for 4 hours. I usually give her about $10.00, if I give her this she may expect it all the time.

Landon: Wait- I insist. It's only proper that the man who dates a woman with children should pay for her sitter. My dad did it when he was dating my mother.

Omunique: Of course he would. She is his wife. This is a whole different situation.

Landon: duh! Earth to Omunique.

Omunique: Oh!! I get it. Your dad is not your real father.

Landon: Well, to me he is. He raised me from the time I was two years old. You know any man can father a child, but not any man can be a father.

Omunique: Boy, do you know, I am a product of a step-father too. As my dad says, there is no such thing as a step-father. A step is something you step on. He is one of the persons responsible for my success today. He wouldn't let me give in when I wanted to. My grandmother was always there too. She was my major inspiration.

Landon: See, another thing we have in common. Here, take this and thank your children for allowing me to spend time with their mother. Tell Diane this is a special gift from me. (kisses her forehead). Talk to you later.

Omunique: Thank you again, Landon. (Exhales really loudly before going into the house).

Landon: God, I don't know what's come over me, but I love it. I know that she is the one.

Scene 15

(It is the next day @ 9:30 a.m).

Landon: (calling Omunique). Good morning, I hope that it is not too early to call, but I wanted to talk to you before you made any plans today. I would like to take you and the boys skating at the beach today, and then maybe we all could stop and get some lunch afterwards. I am going to believe that you will go. I won't take no for an answer.

Omunique: Good morning, Landon I always get up early; with two boys they never sleep late in the morning. I was just thinking about taking them to the beach today. I appreciate your offer, but believe me after one day out with them, you will be running. They are extremely active, and that is an understatement. Besides, I explained to you my policy about having my children exposed to my dates.

Landon: Listen Omunique, before you make another excuse let me say this. I don't plan on hurting you or the boys. We did say we were friends, right?

Omunique: Right.

Landon: Well, if I were a new girlfriend calling and asking you to go to the beach, would you go if you didn't have any other plans?

Omuique: Well, yes, I guess, if I didn't have any other plans.

Landon: Exactly. So why should it be any different because I am a man? It is not like I am asking to spend the night with you, now that is something different. Allow your boys to see how a man should treat a woman, because one day they will be dating. They need to know how a healthy male-female relationship should be.

Omunique: I see now why you are a lawyer. You put up a very good argument. You know, it is interesting, my pediatrician just said the exact thing you said about my exposing my children to dates. He said as long as it is done tastefully, he sees no reason why the boys shouldn't be exposed to good men who treat their mother well. He said that it will give them an example of how to treat women in their lives. Well, you won this case, Counselor.

Landon: Courts adjourned. Let's say I pick you all up about 11:00.

Omunique: Okay, but you better take plenty of vitamins.

Landon: I welcome the challenge with them. I will probably tire them out. I am a big kid at heart. You will see.

Omunique: It's your body(laughs, as they hang up the phone). God this is the first man that I have ever felt this way about. I hope that my feelings are right. Please Lord show me a sign if he is not the right one. I hope that you have finally answered my prayers.

(The phone rings again: It is Landon calling Omunique back).

Landon: Hey Omunique, I forgot to tell you what a wonderful time I had last night. I see so much drive in you. You put a whole new definition on single-mothers.

Omunique: Why thank you. So did I. If I didn't have high expectations for myself, then I would just be another statistic of the system. I want to control my income, not someone else to do it. That is just what the welfare system does. You wait every month for that measly money, that they give you a hard time about getting. It is barely enough to survive on. I know because I've been there. My boys and I deserve better. After all they didn't ask to be born, so why should I make them suffer?

Landon: See, it is that type of attitude I like about you. I know it is difficult raising two boys alone, however, your labor is not in vain. You have done a great job with them so far. You know they say God helps those who help themselves. Well, let me go before we start a whole new conversation.

Omunique: Yes, and you know we both seem to talk quite a bit. See ya (they both hang up the phone).

Omunique: Randolph and Jordan, come on we are going to the beach with a friend of mine. (the boys scream, Yeah)! Remember that guy who brought you guys back to me at the beach?

Randolph: Yes, and we saw him at the restaurant, and he bought us these trucks last night.

Omunique: You don't forget anything do you? Well yes, that is him. He wants to take us out skating and then out to eat.

Jordan: Yeah, I liked him mommie. (Phone rings again).

Omunique: I am never going to get dressed if this phone keeps ringing. Hello?

(Other voice over the phone) Hello Omunique? this is Jacine, Jeff's wife. Since you filed for child-support from him, we will not be sending you anymore money. We are going to fight, so that you will never get even a penny out of us. We have also hired the best attorney in New York. (Jeff gets on the phone) You bitch. You will starve to death before you get anything from me. How dare you have me served(phone clicks).

Omunique: (can't call them back to respond because she doesn't have a number, she starts crying hysterically). Why is it when one thing goes well another goes bad? How am I going to make it until September now?

Randolph and Jordan: Mommie, why are you crying?

Omunique: I just have a cold, go on in the kitchen and finish your breakfast. Would you guys mind very much if we didn't go to the beach today?

Randolph and Jordan: Ah Mommie, we want to go!!

Omunique: Okay, I already told you we would go. (I hope that I can stay composed around Landon).

Landon: (calls back again) Omunique, I know this is my third time calling, but I just wanted to call and say hey, is there something wrong?, you sound like you have been crying.

Omunique: I am allright, thanks for the concern. It's just something personal that came up, and I don't know if I can make it. Maybe another time.

Landon: Wait a minute, what transpired in the last 5 minutes.

Just a moment ago you sounded really elated about going out with me. Omunique, I am your friend. I want to be here to help you. I know that I have just met you, but I can feel your pain. I think that we have connected. Give me a chance to see if I can help, please.

Omunique: I just don't want your sympathy or pity, and I don't want you to think that you are walking into a situation full of troubles right now.

Landon: I would never think that. I am a much bigger person than you give me credit for. Try me. Everyone has their own cross to bear, and if they don't, then something must be wrong with them.

Omunique: I have seen, and experienced so many things that nothing surprises me anymore. I just wish people would start accepting their responsibility. (bursts out crying).

Landon: Whoa, Whoa, what is it sweetie?, Please include me in your pain. I want to help a friend, however, if you don't want my help, I can't force it on you.

Omunique: Well, you know my children's dad has been paying voluntary child support, for about four years now. I promised him and his family that I wouldn't file on him if he sent the payments regularly every month. Well, it got to the point that he was trying to control me with the money. If I wasn't home by a certain time when he called, then no support for weeks. If he called and degraded me, then I would hang up the phone, no child support. I took it for four years until one day I got fed up and decided to take my life back from his control. I filed. He was served recently and that is why I received the phone call. His wife called and said no more child support, and he took the phone and called me names like he always does, and basically said the same thing she did. They hung up the phone before I could reply. It is going to be very difficult making it until September. That is when I start my job, and then I won't want his money.

Landon: He is supposed to be an attorney, a professional. He doesn't handle his life like he is a professional. It goes to show you that if you are full of garbage that is all that can come out of you. He is not even smart enough to know that this is not hurting you, but the children. He has two beautiful black sons who are very intelligent, and with you as their mother they are definitely going to be someone. Then, that is the time he wants to come back and say I am their daddy, when he didn't contribute anything to their development. That is a weak man. Well, we could beat him up all day, but you need a solution. Omunique, I know this may sound personal, but how much was he sending you a month?

Omunique: To be frankly honest he was sending me $2,000.00 a month.

Landon: That is not bad. You know my dad has been looking for a secretary for his office for the summer. Every summer his secretary goes on vacation for two months. We usually have a woman who fills in every summer, but she is getting married. The work is easy; very light typing, and filing, answering the phone and running errands. He was willing to pay her $1,800.00 a month for six hours of work a day. The hours are from 9:00 to 3:00. I know you type, because you are a journalism major, so this would work out well for you. The environment is really fun. Do you think you can do it? It is yours if you want it. I will also see if he has any friends in New York who maybe able to handle your case.

Omunique: Are you serious? I will take it. What a blessing. I can't believe this. I will just have to sacrifice something for a few months on that salary, but we will get through. You are starting to sound like my knight who comes and rescues me. I could have your dad take money out of my salary to pay for my attorney's fees.

Landon: That may work. You know sometimes you have to open up and trust someone, Omunique. Everyone doesn't prejudge you, because of your situation, and those who do are not your friends anyway. My grandmother always said the same measure which you use to judge someone is the same measure which you are being judged. God puts us through our trials and tribulations for a reason. You may not be able to see the reason while you are going through it, but it always manifests itself in the end. You and the boys may suffer right now, but God will never put any more on you than you can bear. You have to be strong for the boy's sake as well as your own. The wheels of justice turn slowly, but in the end you and the boys will be compensated very well.

Omunique: I know that everything you are saying is true, and like Maya Angelou told Oprah you should thank the Lord for whatever you are going through, and I thank you Landon for being here.

Landon: Hey, you don't have to thank me, One day I may need your support. Omunique, I have to be perfectly honest. I really like you and your boys. I want us to develop a friendship and then let the relationship continue to progress to whatever it turns out to be. You have something really special about you on the inside which transcends to the outside. The little child in me wants to explore and see what it is all about. Let me hurry and get dressed to get over there. You need a big hug.

Scene 16

(Brittany calls Khari on the phone).

Brittany: Hello, may I please speak with Khari?

Khari: Speaking. Whom do I have the pleasure of speaking

with?

Brittany:(blushing), This is Brittany. Khari, I had a nice time last night, and I just(pausing)

Khari: I just what? Brittany spit it out, I won't bite you. I promise, or maybe I will depending on what you say.

Brittany: (giggling). I was wondering, if you are not busy today, would you like to go to the beach with me and just walk the boardwalk?

Khari: I explained to you last night that I wasn't interested in being one of your kling-ons. I told you to call me only when you woke up and made up your mind that you make your own decisions in life. You are a grown woman, Brittany, with a lot to offer someone if you will just let go of the chains in your mind that are keeping you from enjoying life to the fullest.

Brittany: Khari, you know until I met you I lived in this bubble and thought the whole world revolved around me, my family, and friends. No one has ever gotten close enough to even try and penetrate my bubble. Now, I meet someone who has made me see that there is a real world out there other than mine and that a lot of times things are not what they always seem in people. It is kind of scary, because it is the uncertainty of not knowing what is really out there in this world.

Khari: You know information reduces uncertainty, that is why I suggested the books, to expose you to other readings. I know it is scary. It is always scary to drift out of your comfort zone, but you know fear is just Fantasizing Events Appearing Real. You, your family and friends are afraid to love the fact that you are black, because you think that it will make the white people love you less. Well Brittany, let me tell you something. How can someone love someone when they don't even love themselves? It is all right to love yourself, be proud of who you are.

Brittany: Khari, you know I have started reading that book, "How to Kill Your Willie Lynch?" and the character in the book sounds a lot like me. I am not that bad, am I? It is funny now that I am thinking about it, it sounds like my life completely so far. I am dying to see what the outcome is.

Khari:(smiling) Girl, I think that you are on your way to opening those eyes. Did you ever have a cold when you were little and it got into your eyes and you couldn't open them because there was so much crust on them?

Brittany: Yes, I did, and it was rather disgusting. No matter how hard I tried to open them, they would not open. So, my mother massaged them with oil until I was able to open them fully on my own.

Khari: Well, it is the same remedy I am using now. You see, your eyes have been closed so long to who and what you are. So, I have to gently massage them like your mother did; only my oil is books and exposing you to the real world. I have to do it gently until you are able to open your eyes yourself.

Brittany: What a wonderful metaphor. You know you are so interesting and intelligent and very unpredictable. It is like the more I talk to you the more I want to get to know you better. I feel like I am becoming addicted to you.

Khari: Why not? I may not be as bad as you think I am.

Brittany: Well, enough of this conversation. Do you want to go to the beach with me or not?

Khari: You know Brittany, whenever I hit to close to home, you always want to change the subject, but that is all right for now. Sure why not go to the beach. Is this a date, or do I meet you again?

Brittany: Why don't you come and pick me up. (she gives him her address, and directions).

Khari: Wow, our first real date(sarcastically) and Brittany I promise not to blow the horn. What time would you like me to pick you up?

Brittany: Please don't get the big head Khari. This is not really a date, it is just an outing for two people to enjoy the sun at the beach.

Khari: (smiling) Why of course it is an outing.

Britt: (laughing) I can tell you have some class, so I am not even worried about you blowing the horn for me. Well I will see you about 11:00.

(Dominique has been secretly listening to Britt's conversation)

Dominique: I happened to over hear some of your conversation. Who is this man you've made a date with? I have never heard you talk to Landon with the enthusiasm you did, with this young man. What type of work does his parents do? Are they in any of our social clubs?

Britt: Mom, first of all I do have other male friends, and this is a man who I met at the beach a couple of days ago. There is something intriguing about him. You may remember him. He was the young man who Rev. O.C. acknowledged for graduating from Cal State, majoring in Engineering. To answer your question about his parents, no, they don't belong to any of your social clubs. I believe they are just blue-collar workers.

Dominique: Now Britt, I can understand you wanting to get a little play out before you get married, but I don't want you to do anything that would jeopardize your relationship with Landon. We worked too hard and long to get you kids to this point. Besides, if you are going to play around with someone, why not make it someone of your same class? Heaven forbid if you fall in love with this low-life ghetto person. His parents are blue-collar workers. What the hell is wrong with you? He went to a Cal-State school? I would rather die first than to see you with a low-life. I can't let it happen again.

Britt: Mom please, everything is always what you want. What if I don't want this relationship with Landon. What if I want to fall in love and be happy with someone I choose for myself? Who cares what type of work his parents do? They are God-fearing people like us. It is good that they at least have a job and are not just on welfare looking for an handout. They just didn't have the advantages you and dad had to send him to an Ivy League School. He is very intelligent; finished Valedictorian in his class. He is a very special person. I am intrigued by him. I want to get to know him better. Besides, I don't love Landon.

Dominique: What the hell does love have to do with it? You will have all the material things to bring you happiness with Landon. Now, I don't want to hear another word about this topic. Yes, he was very good looking, but an Engineer from a Cal-State school just think about what kind of life you would have. You know he won't make as much money as a corporate attorney from an Ivy League school. He would never fit into our world. He would always feel inferior to your world.. Eventually, he would try to take you away from your world and make you fit into his. You would feel resentful because his low-class friends will hate you. They will always think that you think that you are too good to be around them, which would be true. Honey, we are talking about two totally different life-styles; The haves and have nots. This is what distinguishes us from those low-life ghetto blacks. Money wipes away the color of your skin.

Britt: Mom, money and titles of a person is not what makes a person good. It is the individual himself. Everyone is not a product of their environment: It is the true essence of a person that makes them who they are. For your own edification, money does have a color. I thought the same way you did, until I went away to college. I was just a black girl at college. They didn't look at me any differently from the other blacks because I had money. I was miserable for four years, Mom. They had me wear pig-tails and serve them all dressed in an Aunt Jemima outfit while I was on line. The few blacks who attended college with me shook their heads in disgust at me. They didn't want to hang around me, and the whites only invited me to certain functions. What is funny though, the black girls who did come from the ghetto on scholarship were treated better by the whites than I was, because the whites use to say they were so real. I didn't understand, I think I do now. I don't want to live life like this anymore. You know I was just going out with Khari for fun, but now I realize a lot of things he said about me are true. I am a product of you. This conversation has put a whole different twist on things. I am waking up.

Dominique: Listen, you or no one else is going to keep this marriage to Landon from happening. You go out and have your fun with this boy from the hood, and after today, I don't want to hear anything else about him. You are very ungrateful. Do you even realize the sacrifices your dad and I made. We didn't expose you to people like this boy for a reason. He only likes you because you have money. Britt, don't you realize we are not like them. We are different. I can't let your curiosity about a boy from the hood ruin everything we built, and I won't. This must not get out to your father. He would be devastated. You are the only hope to carry on what we have started. You might have had some bad experiences at school, but look at where you are. You pledged one of the finest sororities and you graduated from an Ivy League School. Think about how good that looks on your resume. They didn't let the ghettos girls pledge. Britt, oh my God you must be sick. I just know you are not going out of the house looking like that.

You don't have your contacts in or your wig on. You look like shit, or should I say very ethnic. See he is already destroying you. Look at yourself in the mirror. Honey fix yourself up this very minute before anyone sees you.

Britt: I am not sick, and I am tired of you running my life. I am a woman now. Mother, I hate to disappoint you and Dad, but I am a confused woman. I don't want to live life around people who only accept me to a certain extent because of my economic status. I want to try and see what it would be like around people who are more like me; who love me just because I am me. I get sick and tired of putting these lenses in and putting this wig on. Look at me. I am beautiful like this, even if you think I look ethnic. I look strange the other way, and so do you. Mom, take out your weave and lenses. Oh, about those ghettos girls pledging, they had too much dignity to walk around campus looking like I did.

Dominique: You truly have gone crazy. I am going to call my therapist tomorrow. You have been black-washed and I do mean literally.

(Unbeknownst to both Dominique and Brittany, Michael has been listening to the whole conversation).

Michael: I think that she looks absolutely wonderful. She doesn't look ethnic. This is the person that I brought into the world. I don't know who or what she is the other way. Dominique, why don't you try looking like Britt? I fell in love with you when you looked like her. My God, I forgot how beautiful you were. Brittany is the spitting image of you back then. All the men used to go crazy over that nappy long hair and those big beautiful brown eyes. Now they all laugh. I don't know who or what I am married to now. The girl is right, Dominique. She is woman enough to do what she wants to do. Hon, we already lost one daughter because we tried to do the same thing with her. She has run off and gotten married and we have grandchildren that we haven't even seen. All because she didn't marry that doctor you wanted her to marry and married a policeman instead. I will not lose another daughter. I want her to be happy with her decisions.

Dominique: Got damn you! How dare you even have the audacity to talk to me that way. All you black men are all the same. Once you have made it, you want to go and get a women of the other race. It doesn't matter what her social or economic background is, just as long as she isn't black. So, I am giving you want you want, the eyes and the hair since I wasn't born with them. I know men find me very exotic looking, so I don't know who the hell you are talking about when you say people are laughing. What is going on here? You two have a serious problem. Michael, we are different from those niggers out there. We worked so hard to get to this level, and now you want to feel guilty about not being like those so called people?

Michael: If you only knew the truth, Dominique. All black men don't want a white woman when they make it. More and more of us are realizing that our black sisters are a precious gem. Haven't you noticed that all the women of other races are trying to look like you. They all perm their hair, inject their lips, tan all year around at tanning booths, and now they are even wearing padded jeans. Dear, I think that somewhere you got it all wrong. I want my old Domi back. I know how Brittany felt at college, because I went through the same situation at work. I am all right in the office, but let me try and go to their social clubs or be invited to their homes. I am tired of hearing that I am different from the rest. I am not different, my skin is still black. The only difference is I have money. One thing I realized over the past few years is no matter how much money I have, I am still black in their eyes. I always thought that once I reach this level my skin wouldn't make any difference, but it does. Honey, you must realize this too, before it is too late. I am not saying that we need to go back and live in the hood, but we do owe an obligation to those of us who are working hard to get out of the barrel. If one could pull another up, then it would be a lot easier up at the top. There is strength in numbers. I can't fight this battle alone. I don't want to be a token any longer.

Dominique: Enough of this nonsense, Your other daughter made the decision to marry a blue-collar worker, not me. I have only one daughter now, and I am not going to lose her to this ghetto boy. He probably speaks ebonics. Michael, just because you have had a few bad experiences at work doesn't mean it happened just because you are black. You and Britt are using the same old excuse all these blacks on welfare use. I can't do this, or go here because of the white man, Get off of it both of you. Since we are on the subject, I would appreciate it if you don't bring that low-life Mustafa around here anymore. He is so ethnic. I can't believe you hired him. Every since you have been hanging around him you have been acting like a low-life black person. I know he is putting all this bull-shit in your head, because he is jealous of you. He is one of those who tries to make you feel guilty about making it. I don't want the neighbors talking, so keep him away. I am going to have my nails and hair done, and then I am meeting Landon's mom at the caterer. Don't let me have to call Landon. TTFN. (As she walks out of Britt's room turns to her husband)how dare you humiliate me in front of our child? You know she looks like a piece of shit.

Michael: Before you go dear, let me explain to you why I hired Mustafa. He out-ranked all the other applicants. They were all white, get that. He is a very spiritual person, one of the best person I've met in a long time. There is no phoniness about him. He may not have learned to speak English the proper way like we do, or know all the proper etiquette, but he is still a good man and I like him. He loves who he is and his black people as well. Believe it or not, the whites really like him because he is real. They respect him a whole lot more than they have ever respected me. I have learned a lot from this man, and I will not give up his friendship. To hell with what people think about him. If only people would have half a heart as good as he does, then this world would be a much better place. So go on and get all your fake nails and hair done, but remember no matter how white you try to look, you are still black. Now TTFN on that dear!!!!

Dominique: You black bastard, we have not finished with this. I have to go, but you better be ready for me when I return. Both you and your daughter sound like the poor-me niggahs. I will not have that type of mentality in my household.

Michael: No, we haven't finished, and I think you better be ready for me when I returned. You know what's funny? you called me a black bastard. It is just like the whites. I can't just be a bastard, I have to be a black bastard.

Dominique: Whatever, I am out of here. You are sick.

(Meanwhile, back in Brittany's room).

Britt:(crying) Oh, I need to call Landon, and tell him that I am going to be busy so that he doesn't drop by(picks up the phone to call Landon). Hello Landon.

Landon: Hey Britt.

Britt: It is Brittany please.

Landon Well excuse me, I thought that you always liked being called Britt. I was just about to call you.

Britt: Before you finish, any plans that you have made for us today, I can't make it. I have other plans for today.

Landon: Well that's funny I was just about to tell you the same thing. Have a nice day.

Brittany: You too.

Landon: Brittany, maybe later on this evening we can get together. We really need to talk about some things that have been bothering me. We need to make some decisions about our relationship.

Brittany: Boy, you must be clairvoyant today, because I have been thinking along the same lines (they both hang up the phone).

Landon: Man, that was too easy. Something is not right; and call me Brittany, not Britt. What's up with that? Oh well probably another one of her changes she's going through.

Michael: Brittany, I just want you to know that I am behind you 100 percent, and I will deal with the witch if this is what you really want. Go for it.

Britt: (hugs dad's neck) Thanks, and oh you called me Brittany, matter of fact you have always called me Brittany.

Michael: That is what I named you, not Britt. People have to live up to their name.

Britt: Hey, that is what Khari said (smiles).

Michael: Well, I am off to hit a few balls, and remember pumpkin if we have to throw hot water on the wicked witch to kill her, we will (both of them laugh).

Britt: How have you put up with her all these years?

Michael: The same way I put up with you. I am happy to see that you are finally opening your eyes, because believe me, no man wants a bitch. Your mother wasn't always the way she is now. The more money we made the more she became a different person. I don't even remember when she stopped looking and being black. I love you Brittany and I don't want to see you end up like your mother. Go out and live. Well, I am out of here.

Britt: I love you too Dad, I love you(hugs him). Dad, by the way, have you ever really had real soul-food.

Michael: Why yes, I go to the Café Avenue at least once a week. If your mother knew she would die. There are a lot of other things I do culturally that your mother doesn't know.

Britt: Well, I went the other day to the Cafe Avenue with a friend and I loved it.

Michael: Get out of here. Brittany, since we are talking, now that you are out of college I plan on leaving your mom. I want a down to earth black woman. I miss my roots. I feel like I am a black man trapped in a white's man body. Believe me honey, no real black man wants a bitch or phony black woman. I have been seeing this woman for three years, and she makes me remember when once upon a time it was nice to be black. I am not going to play golf either. I am going to a Bid-wist party with her. I haven't played that in years.

Britt: Wow, talking about dropping the bomb on me. What will Mother do? And when were you going to tell me about it?

Michael: Believe me, your mother will be very well taken care of. She can keep the house and I have arranged for her to continue to live the life-style she is accustomed to. I don't have very many more years for happiness, and I want to enjoy them. You never know what tomorrow holds, and yesterday is like a canceled check; it is gone forever. By the way, after I saw how happy your sister was, something clicked in my head. It is not about status or material things that brings a person happiness. It is being in love with that person. I see your sister and her family once a week. They are one of the happiest couples I know. They love my lady friend also.

Britt: Boy, you certainly have been living a double life. This is a hard pill to swallow. Well, we will talk later. Have a great day Pops.

Michael: I will, but remember follow your heart and not your pocket book for love. Keep opening up your eyes.

Scene 17

Katrina: Landon, I just happened to be walking by and heard you make a date. It sounds like with a woman with children, and then I heard you break a date. with Brittany. What is going on? I know you can't be serious. I understand you have been under a lot of stress, getting ready to start working in our family's law firm and preparing to take the bar. I know these things can sometimes cause you to act out of character. You sure that you didn't get involved in drugs while you were in college?

Landon: Mom, calm down. I am not stressed. I didn't do drugs, and yes, the girl I am taking out has two children, and yes I did break my date with Brittany. This woman is very educated, a good mother, and she has substance. She is not fake, inconsiderate, stuck-up, wannabe,stressful, bitchy or any of the other adjectives I could go on and name that describe Britt. This woman is like a breath of fresh air. Britt is someone you chose for me when I was a kid. I did a lot of thinking while I was away at college, and I realized that I didn't want to marry someone who someone else picked for me. I wanted to fall in love and know that I picked the person myself. You think I want someone like Britt to be the mother of my children?

Katrina: Landon, that is why we brought you up with the finest things in life and sent you to the finest schools, so that you would be exposed to people more like yourself. You and this woman would have nothing in common, but this so called love.

You know love, is a very volatile emotion. What happens when the love wears out. Will she even know how to act at all the different affairs you will be going to. Britt was raised in that type of world. She has the proper etiquette and social graces for your world. She will compliment you.

Landon: Mom, this young lady is educated. She will be working as a journalist for a major network. Can you imagine how many different types of people she is going to encounter in her everyday life? A major network wouldn't just hire anyone to work there knowing that they couldn't deal with the many facets of people she is going to encounter. She may not have attended an Ivy league school, but the fact is she has aspirations and is fulfilling them. Yes, she is a mother, but that doesn't negate the fact that she isn't a person first. Besides, you act like I am ready to marry her. I just know she is like a breath of fresh air compared to the women I have been brought up around.

Katrina: What if you really started getting serious about this woman? You know the more you hang around someone, the easier it is for you to get attached to them and children are really easy to get attached to. You know she already has two children, now heaven forbid if you have anymore together. You will never get ahead. Why would you even entertain the thought of possibly getting serious with this woman? I think that we need to call Britt and her mother over so that we can all sit down and talk and work this thing out.

Landon: We don't need to do any such thing. You know the days of your running my life is over, Mom. I appreciate all that you and dad have done for me, but now it is my life. I respect you as my Mom, but you have to respect me as your son as well as a man. I can't believe I am hearing this come from out of your mouth. Did you forget where you came from? You know Dad took you in when I was only two years old. You know the hell you went through with his parents and friends.

Unlike Omunique, you didn't even have an education. Dad put you through school. So from the start, she has a lot going for her than you ever did. Just think about it. What if Dad was not his own man, and didn't stand up for what he wanted? You told me they had already picked out the woman for him to marry. You and I wouldn't even be here today if he had given in to all the pressure.

William: (walks into room). You know Katrina, the boy, excuse me, I mean the man, is totally right. I will not stand here and let him be controlled by anyone. He has a right to pick whomever he wants to marry. What have we become. We promised ourselves that if we ever made it we would go back to the community and help others who were less fortunate, but we have gotten so comfortable up here on the hill, that we don't even think about anything else. There is a whole world down there and if we don't start taking care of our own and trying to get others up here with us, then it will be easy to take us out when they get tired of us. There is strength in numbers, and there are only a few of us who they say have so called made it. I am tired of playing the white man's game. I want to be me and be happy like we once were. I am in no way preaching hatred against anyone, but love of ourselves and our own comes first.   We have bought into that adage: "What's love got to do with it". Well it has a lot, and that is why I married you, Katrina..

Katrina: You know, you two are right. I have always hated this pretentious life. Honey I always thought you enjoyed it, so I played along and played along well. I never knew you felt the same way too.

William: I did it because I thought it was what you always wanted. Your self-esteem was so low when I came along and rescued you. You always talked about how you wanted the house on the hill; to have social parties, the finest cars and etc. etc. So I gave you these things to try and raise your esteem.

Katrina: Yes, at one time I thought I did want it. I still do, but how can I be happy knowing that there are other people in my race who would just love a taste of some of this. It is our obligation to help, if not all, at least one other person out of the ghetto. We need to show the kids that there is hope and that it can be done through education and hard work. Landon, if you really feel in your heart that this woman is good, and not just trying to use you, then my blessings are with you. I think that we raised you well enough to make good decisions. You have never disappointed us yet. I just want the best for you(they all hug). By the way, to be truthfully honest, I have never, ever cared for Britt and her mother. I don't know how her husband managed to stay with her. He is totally different when he is away from them.

William: Well that situation with Dominique and Michael will be changing too. This doesn't leave our house. You hear you two?

Landon: Man, look at the time, I have to go and pick Omuningue and the children up. By the way, Dad, are you still looking for someone to help for the summer in the office? The reason I asked is because Omunique's children's dad just decided that he isn't going to send her money for the children. She had him served by the District Attorney. She is also willing to let you take part of her salary to hire an attorney to represent her. Do you have any connections in New York?, because the father lives in New York.

William: The answer to your first question is yes I am still looking, and I will give her an interview. If I like her I will hire her. The answer to your second question is yes, I do have a great family attorney who can possibly help her whether I hire her or not. He owes me a big favor. You know how I feel about dead beat dads.

Katrina: I hope that we can help her with her legal matters, especially when it comes to child-support. That is a dirty shame. Omunique what an unusual name. She must be unique for you to like her. How old are the children?, and what are their names?

Landon: Randolph is 5 and Jordan is 3. They are both extremely intelligent boys, and very handsome. You may have seen them the other day in church when she stood up for graduating from Cal-State, and the Rev. said how she did it with two children. The irony of her dilemma is the fact that the children's dad is an attorney

Katrina: Oh my gosh!!, I remember that young lady. She has been on my mind lately. I noticed her in the restaurant and there was just something different and unique about her. I really admired her. She is also very pretty. Well, go and send our regards, and we look forward to meeting her and the boys soon. Guess what? I am supposed to meet (Britt's mom) at the caterer, I can't wait to see the expression on her face when I tell her that there has been a change of plans.

Landon: Mom, I know how much you would love to just burst her bubble, but wait and let me do it the right way with Britt. Just call or page her and tell her that you can't make it today because an emergency came up.

Katrina: Okay, if you insist, but yes you are right in handling the situation with Britt first.

William: Katrina, since we are having a lot of new developments in the family today, I need to tell you that I have been involved with this mentoring program in the inner-city for our black-youths. I am meeting with some of them today. Would you like to join me? You would be a great mentor for the teenage moms.

Katrina: Wow, you guys is there anything else I need to know? Believe it or not, I have been contemplating doing something like that. I suggested to the girls in my social club about mentoring to the less fortunate, but they all thought that it was ridiculous. Honey, I wouldn't miss it for the world.

William: Sweetheart, this is just great. I feel I have my old lady back. I just have one request before we go. Can you get rid of the blonde wig and contact lenses? I want to see the look that attracted me to you once upon a time.

Katrina: You mean you don't like this look? And all the time I thought that this was what you wanted. I hate looking like this. I feel like I am a wanna-be. Whenever I go off by myself and no one is around, I wear my own hair and no darn lenses. I am too black to have green eyes. Wait one minute, I had my hair done under here this morning.

William: Boy, Landon we really need to start communicating again. We were lost, but now I think we have found the right path again.

Katrina: How do you like me now?

Landon and William: Wow!! Is that really you? You are absolutely gorgeous.

William: Come on here woman. I want to take you and show all my friends my beautiful black woman. From here on out we are black and we are proud, and no more lack of communication. Agreed.

Landon and Katrina: Agreed. (They all hug).

Scene:18

(Landon arrives at Omunique's house. He rings the door bell).

Omunique: Come on in through the garage(lets the garage door up).

Landon:(Sees a Honda and a Blazer in the garage). Hey if you have company, I can come by later.

Omunique: No, I don't have company. Both cars are mine. I just purchased the Blazer because the boys and I wanted one....

Landon: To be a single-mom, you certainly have it going on. I am impressed more and more every time I see you. I shouldn't have expected anything less. What a nice place inside.

Omunique: I try. It takes a while to decorate a house, after moving from a town-house. I am just leasing it, so I am only going to do so much. Once my income gets better, I plan on buying a home for us.

Randolph and Jordan: (both jump from behind the couch and try to scare Landon. They both yell rah!!)

Landon: Oh I am scared. Please, don't hurt me. Are you boys ready to head to the beach?

Boys: Yeah, we are going skating.

Jordan: Do you have any children?

Landon: No, what about you?

Randolph: He can't have any children, he is still a baby.

Landon: I know, I was just kidding. Do you boys know how to skate, and do you have all your gear?

Boys: Yes, our mommie bought everything.

Landon: By the way, Omunique, I spoke to my dad today. He is really interested in you. He would like to interview you for the position. I can't help you there, but I know you will do well. He will fall in love with you. He also has a friend who is an attorney in New York. He owes my dad big time, so regardless if you get the job or not, my dad is going to help you. He despises dead-beat dads. My parents are dying to meet you and the boys. They feel that I make good decisions, so they know you must be special like your name.

Omunique: (hugs Landon's neck). Thank you God, and thank you Landon. I have all the faith in the world that everything is going to work out. I am not going to wait till the battle is over to shout. I am going to shout now for victory(screams). Okay everybody, let's go (they put kids in car and fasten the seat belts).

Boys: We like your car

Landon: Thank you.(turns and looks at Om). You look great.

Omunique: (fighting backs tears) Thank you. I am looking forward to meeting your parents. They sound like great people. I was expecting the worst once they found out about me.

Landon: How could they? My dad remembers what it was like when he wanted to marry my mother, and she had me to bring to the picture also. A startling thing happened at home before I arrived to pick you up. My mom got rid of her blonde wig and green lenses today, and she looked wonderful. I still can't believe how beautiful she is. She wants to go back to being black 100%.

(Landon and the boys are singing while driving to the beach. Om is impressed that Landon knows all the songs the boys do. She remains pretty quiet during the ride).

Scene 19

(Khari arrives at Brittany's house. He is amazed at how big and beautiful the house is).

Khari: Wow, I didn't even imagine that we own houses as big as this. Boy, she really is an elitist. Now, I can understand a little better why she thinks the way she does. She is an absolute product of her environment.

Khari: (rings bell a butler answers the door). Your name isn't Jeffrey is it? (the butler starts to laugh, he says his name is Andre).

Andre: You are a real brother(gives him the handshake) Boy,

living up here all week with these phony blacks makes you appreciate the hood even more. You must be Khari. Ms. Britt is expecting you. She has been checking every 5 minutes for your arrival. Don't tell her I told you that. Have a seat. Will you care for something to drink?

Khari: No, why yes I changed my mind. I just want to see how it feels getting served by a butler.

Andre: No problem Master Khari.

Khari: Hey man don't start that. I am no one's master but my own, and there is only one master for all of us. That is God, and I am not a God the last time I checked.

Andre: I was just kidding. I don't call anyone master but the Lord also. Word.

Khari: Word.

Brittany: Oh Khari, you made it. I guess I must have given you pretty good directions.

Khari: To say the least. I had to check my Thomas Guide to get here. You told me left when I should have gone right, and right when I should have gone left. I made it, so no sweat. This is a great pad. Boy, I did not know they let us brothers live up this high.

Britt: It will do. I have seen bigger. Well, are you ready to hit the beach?

Khari: Yeah let's go. Oh Andre, forget about the drink. If I get a chance to return, then I will let you do me up.

Andre: Sure thing Khari, and remember, my brother, stay black.

Khari: Always, and the same too goes for you.

Britt: Why Andre, I have never heard you talk like that.

Andre: That is because I have never ran into a real brother up here except for Mustafa. We usually talk in private, so that we won't offend anyone(Turns and walks away).

Britt: What's his trip. Let's go. We can take my car, and let the top down.

Khari: No, we will take my car and I will open the sunroof if you want wind.

Britt: (hesitantly) Oh all right, but it won't be as fun.

Khari: We will make it fun.

Scene 20

(Landon, Omunique and the children arrive at the beach, and skate.. They all are laughing and having fun. It has been three hours and they are ready to leave the beach).

Randolph: Mommie look, that man looks like uncle Khari!!(as the boys see a side view of him)

Omunique: Why it is Khari!!

Landon: If I didn't know any better I would say that woman looks like Britt from the butt. Nah, that can't be her. Look at the woman, she is having to much fun to be Britt. Besides, Britt has blonde hair, I mean a wig.

(Omunique and the children scream: Khari. Britt and Khari turn around and they both are in shock. The boys run to Khari and jump on him).

Brittany:(walks up to Landon and Omunique) So, you bastard, this is what you meant when you said you had other plans. So I see you would rather have a ready made family!

Landon: Excuse me Miss. I don't believe I know you. Have we met some where?

Brittany: Cut the krap, Landon. This is Britt. You know, your fiancee.

Landon: What the hell? You, you, you look awesome. What happened?

Brittany: It doesn't matter. Answer my question! Is this the reason you have been breaking our dates lately? (pointing at Omunique and children).

Landon: You have the nerve to talk. So these were your plans to spend the day out at the beach with someone else. You may have changed your outside appearance, but you are still messed up on the inside. I feel sorry for you.

Omunique: You know Brittany, I was very tactful last time when you said something about me, but this time I am going to stoop all the way to your level. First of all my family is ready made with a lot of love, something which you couldn't possibly know about. You may be this Ms. Buppie Bourgeois person but you change your panty hoses the same way I do, or is it so far up the crack of your butt, you can't pull it out.(she says under her breath). Lord please forgive me, but I lost control.

Britt: Landon, are you going to let her stand there and talk to me that way? Come on Landon, let's leave right now. This woman is just looking for someone to be a father to her children, and for you to rescue her from the ghetto. She also has a very foul mouth.

Khari: (walks up and hears the conversation). Man, was I ever whack thinking that there was some good in you. You know you may have money and a fine house and cars, but you have no class. That is something your parents couldn't buy for you. You wouldn't even understand why your man is with my cousin. Let me break it down for you. My cousin has personality, self-esteem, consideration for other people's feelings, and most of all she respects herself. These are some attributes that a man looks for in a woman. They got your man. Yes, my cousin is looking for a father for her children, but not in the aspect you think she is. What single mother wouldn't look for a good man? It is not her fault that Landon likes her. Come on Om, let's get out of here. And man you can have her. I don't need or want someone like her in my life. I feel sorry for you, my brother.

Landon: Hold on Khari. I came with Omunique and the children so I will leave with them. And Britt, he is right, your attitude, inconsideration and stubbornness are just some of the few things that made me go out looking for someone else. She wasn't looking for me, I was looking for someone like her, I would rather take a woman with 50 children who have the attributes that Omunique, has than to be with someone like you. You know nothing about this woman and have the nerve to judge her. Try looking in the mirror at yourself before you start throwing darts at people.

Omunique: Well, we can't leave the child here by herself.

Brittany: You know what, all you low-life people can leave. I told you Landon the other day when you all went over to play volleyball with them," if you lay down with dogs, you get up with fleas". Boy was I ever right. I will have my butler pick me up, and another thing, Landon I hate you. I have never loved you anyway. Boy, will your parents eat her up alive when you bring her home.

Landon: Just one last thing for your own edification, Brittany, my parents are looking forward to meeting her and the boys. But I am not going to stand here and stoop to your level by saying things that will hurt you, like you are so famous for doing.

Khari: Omunique let me take the boys, I believe you and Landon need to talk alone. Call or page me when you are ready for me to bring them home. Boys, how about going to Discovery Zone?

Boys: Yeah!!

Omunique: Thank you Khari, that is why I love you. (she walks over to Britt) You know my cousin is really a nice guy. He never calls a woman outside of her name no matter how mad he may get at her. He really believes the black man should respect and keep the black woman happy for all the struggles she has been through and what she is going through. He has a whole hell of lot going for him. Just because he isn't an Ivy league graduate or live in the hills doesn't make him any less of a man. You might want to reconsider getting to know him.

Britt: So that you can move me out of the way to take my man. You are crazy. He will come running back. You just wait and see. You have no idea about how to live in our world.

Omunique: You know I am not going to stand here and engage in verbal combat with you. You are not even worth it. I already participated in your combat once, but I won't again. I will not allow you to steal my light from me ever again. Just so you will know, I didn't take your man from you because I know how hard it is to find a decent black man. It just happened.

Landon:(yells over at Omunique) Come on Omunique lets go!) There is no sense trying to talk to her. She will only say mean things to try and hurt and degrade you. You don't need that. (turns to Khari) Khari, I have no intention of using your cousin or her children. I like them a whole lot, and if it doesn't work out, it won't be because of me going back to Brittany. I don't usually fail at my endeavors, and I plan on making this relationship work. The feeling is there.

Khari: I think that I know that. If you were, just having a good time with my cousin, you wouldn't had done what you did with Brittany back there. I look at a person's action, I don't even hear their words until I know that person is credible, because anybody can talk the talk. You know, I have been trying to get Brittany to open her eyes by exposing her to different black books and places. She was really reading them and I could see she was coming around. She may still be Allright, I just think this situation with you and my cousin might be the thing to really have her face reality. I just want you to know I wasn't trying to move in on your turf, even though she does peak my interest.

Landon: No need to explain man, Omunique told me you try to help our people love themselves as well as our people. I was telling her how I wish that you could help Brittany. I know you have a little bit. She finally got rid of that silly wig and blue contact lenses. Just the fact that she is out with you says a lot. Don't get me wrong, I am in no way trying to put you down. It's just that Brittany...

Khari: Listen man, no need to explain. I understand what you are trying to say, that I am not the type of guy she usually would go out with. I am very cognizant of that.

Landon: Wait a minute, something just hit me. Did you and Britt go to the Cafe Avenue the other day? Omunique and I were looking for a parking space when I said to her, that looks like Britt's car. I immediately said no way. She wouldn't be caught in a place like this. We went around the corner and came back, and the car was gone, so we took the space.

Khari: Why, yes we did. What a coincidence. Just think if we had ran into you all there?

Landon: Man, you have made a major break-through. Believe me, I know. There might be hope for the old girl after all. So do you plan on seeing her again?

Khari: I don't know man. Anyone who can put people down like she can has no place in my life. She would really have to change that aspect of herself, and then love herself and her people. She might not be willing to do that.

Landon: I think she may. I still can't believe how good she looks. If only you can fix up the inside now. I was where she is at one time in my life and I am still working on myself. So, if you decide to continue to see her, just be patient.

Boys: Come on Uncle Khari.

Khari: Okay boys, kiss your mom bye-bye. Hey Landon maybe we can talk later.

Landon: Omunique, I apologize for you having to go through this. I had no idea that she was going to be here.

Omunique: Oh, don't worry about it. I was rather surprised myself to see that Khari is going out with her. I would've never figured him to be seeing someone like her. He must really see something good in her.

Landon: Om, maybe it is just like I see something good in you. I am so happy that I met you (pulls her to him and kisses her).

Both: Wow!!!!

Scene 21

(Brittany is sitting on a bench crying and looking at the ground with her cellular phone in her hand).

Britt: I don't need any of them anyway. Mom always said that Landon's dad wasn't his real dad and that deep down inside he might be classless. Boy, was she ever right. He probably feels more at home with someone like her. You can take the man out the ghetto, but you can't take the ghetto out of the man.

Khari: (turns back with boys to walk over to bench where Britt is sitting). Hey Brittany, I brought you here, and no matter what you have done and said to my cousin, I can't just leave you here alone. You came with me so you will leave with me, and after I take you home you can forget all about me. So bite your pride, and come on.

Jordan: Why is she crying Uncle Khari? Would you like to go to Discovery Zone with us?

Randolph: Yeah, it always makes us happy. You will stop crying when you get there. It is so much fun.

Jordan: Yes, it sure is, hum Randolph?

Randolph: I already said that.

Khari: It is fun, and you need to not take life so seriously. Come with us.

Jordan: (Takes Brittany's hand) Come on.

(Britts is laughing now).

Randolph: I know your name is Brittany.

Jordan: Me too.

Britt: How do you know that?

Randolph: Because Uncle Khari said let's go ask Brittany to come with us.

Britt: (looks at Khari). After all that went down a few minutes ago, you are willing to still be nice to me.

Khari: I don't trip on people because we all are human and fall short sometimes. You just haven't learned how to respect other people's differences and feelings. I can't blame you, because you are a product of your environment. It is just unfortunate. I know that deep down in you, you want to be good. I saw a little light shining for a moment. It was rather faint, but I saw it (laughs).

Brittany: You are the first person who has ever treated me like this, and I appreciate it. Several times you could have walked away. Thank you for believing in me, when I don't even believe in myself.

Khari: Let's get going, the boys are getting restless. (they all walk away with Brittany holding the boy's hands).

Scene 22

(Omunique and Landon are riding home).

Landon: I still feel bad about what happened back there at the beach. That was not the way I wanted to settle everything with Brittany. I would've left with her if she hadn't been such a witch, because I knew she was hurting. She has never seen me with another person. I still have to put some closure on the relationship the right way. I was going to do it this evening, but I think that I will let things cool off first. (takes Omunique's hand). I know that I made the right decision though to choose you.

Omunique: Well, I hope that she is all right. She looked beautiful. That doesn't negate the fact that she really has no people skills or tact. I thought that you were exaggerating about her character. I just can't imagine anyone in our society having modern day racism against their own. Our fore-fathers worked too hard so that we wouldn't have so much division and hatred among ourselves. Here you have a beautiful black girl that hates her skin and looks. She doesn't even realize that all women are dying to look like us. They enlarged their lips, bust, and butts, and don't talk about them tanning and perming their hair. These things are considered beautiful on them, but on us it is considered ethnic on us, it is unattractive. We need to wake up and start observing what is really going on.

Landon: You know you are exactly right. I never noticed that before. There were people in my class who went to tanning booths every day in the winter to keep their skin brown and some of their perms were so overprocessed it looked like a white person with nappy hair.

Omunique: Well, there was one good thing about the whole incident today.

Landon: What's that?

Omunique: That kiss, it was really powerful.

Landon: And how (they both laugh and kiss again).

Scene 23

(Khari, the boys, and Brittany are at Discovery Zone. They are all playing in the apparatus, laughing and having fun).

Khari: Come on, boys, let's get going. It is getting late.

Boys: All right (they are tired).

Khari: Brittany, would you watch the children while I go and get our shoes? Can you handle it?

Brittany: Why, of course. I think that me and the boys will be all right. Go ahead. (Brittany is laughing and talking to the boys and is amazed at how intelligent they are. Khari returns with the shoes).

Brittany: Khari, your cousin has done this all by herself? I am very impressed. She has done a fantastic job.

Khari: Yes she has. She is one of the greatest women I know and I mean that.

Brittany: I really have pre-judged her incorrectly. I always had this illusion about single mothers, being on welfare, no ambitions, lazy, and having illiterate children. I have only judged everything from what I have seen on television. I have never actually been exposed to any single mothers. I do owe your cousin a big apology, there is no way in the world I could have survived, if it were me in the same situation.

Khari: I can't fault you Brittany. You are just a product of your environment, but it would be a fault if you didn't really find out about the real world. I think that you are on your way. About apologizing to Omunique, well, you can get your chance if you really mean it. Go with me to take the children home, by the way Landon may be there.

Brittany: That's all right. Landon and I were through a long time ago. We were staying together more for our parents. They thought that we would look good on paper and to society. My ego was hurt more than anything else the fact of seeing him with another woman. I always thought that I had so much control over him, but I guess he proved me wrong.

Scene 24

(Khari and Brittany arrive at Omunique's house).

Brittany: This is her house. This is really nice. This is a nice neighborhood too. I am impressed, I see Landon is still here.

Khari: Yeah, cuz does all right for herself. She doesn't settle for anything (turns around to look at boys. They are asleep). Uh, oh Brittany, I hope that you have muscles. We need to carry them in. You take the little one, Jordan, and I will take Randolph.

Brittany: I think that I can handle that. You sure your cousin is not going to claw my eyes out.

Khari: If I thought that, I wouldn't have brought you here. My cousin is above that level. She is not violent. She handles situations very diplomatically, however she is not going to let anyone just walk all over her(he hands Brittany Jordan and takes Randolph, he rings the bell).

Omunique (answers the door). Khari, what the heck is going

on here. How could you dare bring this woman to my house? Are you crazy?

Khari: Chill out Om. It's all right. Brittany has something that she wants to say to you. You have to realize she was hurt and mad when she saw her fiancee with another woman. You have to understand her feelings too.

Omunique: I understand her feelings, but not the things which she said. There is no excuse for her attacking my character because I am a single mother.

Brittany: You are exactly right. I apologize for pre-judging you. I had no idea what a remarkable person you are. I wish that I could take those words back, but I can't. So let us just move forth from this day because it looks like we may be seeing each other. I really like your cousin(looks at Khari). Don't worry about me and Landon, we have both known the truth all the time about our relationship. It is just neither one of us wanted to be the first to say it. Ahhh, Jordan, here is kind of getting heavy. Can I put him down somewhere?

Omunique: Yes, follow me. I can take him. He is kind of heavy.

Brittany: You have done a great job of raising them alone. They are very intelligent and very mannerable little men.

Omunique: Why thank you. Did you expect anything less from a single mother. I am sorry, that was not nice. Like you said, let us leave the past behind (they lay the children down, and go into the den).

Landon: (comes from out of the restroom) What the hell are you doing here Brittany? How did you get here. Are you all right Omunique?

Khari: Calm down my brother, Everything is cool. Brittany has come to her senses. After you two left, the boys and I went and asked her to join us at Discovery Zone. I don't care how badly she talked to my cousin. I brought her to the beach, I couldn't leave her there. Brittany wanted to come here with me to bring the boys home so that she could apologize to Om. Besides man, I really like her. I hope that it is all right with you. (looks at Brittany).

Brittany: I had the time of my life at Discovery Zone. I can't wait to go again.

Landon: What is this Brittany is saying? I have never seen this side of you, and you apologize? Someone slap me, I do believe that I am dreaming. And to answer your question Khari, no, I don't mind you liking Brittany. It appears you are just the man she needed to bring out the best in her, because I certainly couldn't do it.

Khari: You know these past few days have been a ball of confusion for all of us. Wouldn't you say? (everyone says yeah).

Omunique: Brittany, I didn't thank you for bringing the boys home asleep (everyone laughs). Would you and Khari like to join us to watch Farrakhan's Million Man's March? I was getting ready to prepare some hot wings and Margaritas. The March will be on in about an hour and a half.

Khari: I was going home to watch it with Eric and the gang but if you insist I am game. Is it all right if they come over Om?

Omunique: Of course they can come over. You know me. Brittany hasn't said if she wanted to stay or not.

Brittany: I guess I would like to see what's going on with this Million Man's March. I was just going to disregard it a couple of days ago, but now I really would like to see it. The answer to your question is yes, I would love to see it.

Khari: Brittany, could you do me a favor and call your girlfriend Kolby and have her come over? I promised my friend, Eric, that I would put in a good word for him and arrange for him to meet her again.

Brittany: That is funny. Kolby is interested in him also. She tried to bribe me into telling you that she liked him.

(Everyone makes their phone calls. Each person invites their friends).

Khari: Omunique, you don't have to make anything. Eric and the gang already have everything.

Om: Cool, now I don't have to cook (ha ha).

Brittany: My friends are bringing some things too. I guess we have a full-fledged party here.

Landon: I couldn't get in touch with Lance. Brittany, did you talk with him today?

Brittany: Matter of fact, I did. He said he had a date with some new girl.

Landon: And he didn't even tell me. Hey!, I just thought about it, won't all our friends go berserk when they see what is going on?

Omunique: To say the least. My girlfriend Tanika is bringing her new friend over to meet me. They were going to watch the March with me. The only thing I know about her friend is that he went to Columbia. She is being very secretive.

Scene 25

(Everyone starts arriving. They are all reacquainting themselves with each other. They are all in shock about the relationships that have developed. Everyone is wondering where Lance and Tanika is. Door bell rings).

Omunique: (answers the door). Hey, Tanika where in the hell have you been? I have been waiting for you. The March, starts in about five minutes.

Tanika: Om, we were having so much fun that we lost track of time. My new friend went back to the car to get the drinks. We had no idea that a party was going on. He says a lot of the cars look likes his friend's cars. Is there something going on here?

Omunique: Well you are about to be in for the shock of your life

Lance: (walks up). Hey sweetie and kisses her. Hi Omunigue remember me? Hey, What is really going on? Those are all my friend's cars out there (pointing outside).

Omunique: Boy, Tanika you didn't tell me it was Landon's best friend you have been seeing.

Tanika: I know, I wanted to surprise you.

Omunique: Well we have a lot of talking to catch up on, come on in.

(They walk into the den, and everyone just burst, out laughing and shaking their heads).

Lance: (Rushes over to Landon). What the hell is going on?

Landon: Man we have a lot of talking to do. Later.

Brittany:(walks in between both of them). Landon can I talk to you outside please?

Landon: Sure. (They both walk outside).

Omunique: (walks back into the den from the kitchen, she looks around and sees Brittany and Landon are gone. She assumes they have left together). Everyone can see the look in her eyes and gets sad.

Khari: (walks over and hugs her). We will always have each other no matter what. I guess we drew them both together again. Que sera sera. We will get over it. We are fighters, not quitters.

(Brittany and Landon walk back in together, they both appear to have been crying).

Brittany: I have an announcement to make. Landon and I are officially UN-engaged. (she holds up finger) see, no ring(she hands ring to Landon).

Landon: Brittany you keep it as a souvenir. I can't give it to another woman. Let it be a momento of a band that would have bonded two people together who were not really in love with each other. And to all my friends, I would advise all of you to not buy into what our parents have been selling us. Be your own person. Love whomever makes you truly happy (Walks over and hugs Omunique).

Brittany: Ditto, if I can change anybody can. Boy you all know my mother, she will probably have a breakdown, but she will get over it with a little smelling salt (everyone laughs).

Lance: Is that Brittany? wow! I can't believe it.

Brittany: Yes it is me, and thanks to Khari (hugs him) I am beginning to see the light. I still have a long way to go before I reach the end of the tunnel, but I am willing to try!

Khari: The March is starting everyone get in your places and quiet in the house.

Lance: This whole thing is a ball of confusion. Someone talk to me now!!

Scene 26

(Farrakhan: is speaking about Willie Lynch. Everyone is crying and reflecting on their individual Willie Lynch).

Landon: I hope that all black people wake up and do the right thing and lynch their Willie Lynches, before the others start lynching us again. We all need to take the noose from around our necks. We've had it on 286 years too long.

Everyone says Amen.

Note: Since the publication of my book, attacks on Blacks have started again, or have they ever stopped? Recall the incident in Jasper, Texas?

We must first change ourselves, before trying to change others. Can we finally do it?   We all are made in the image of God. Always let the God in you salute the God in others, then what a wonderful world this would be !!!

Modern Day Willie Lynches:
1. Dark-skinned people are uglier than light-skinned people.
2. Light-skinned people are smarter than dark-skinned people.
3. Dark-skinned people are all on welfare, and are lazier than light skinned people.
4. Dark-skinned people have ethnic features.
5. Black people hate the fact that they are black, so they marry someone of another race to disassociate themselves from being black.
6. Dark-skinned men's genitalia are anatomically larger than light - skinned men.
7. Dark-skinned people are genetically designed better than light- skinned people.
8. Light-skinned blacks have better hair than dark-skinned blacks.
9. Light-skinned blacks smell better than dark-skinned people.
10. Light-skinned people are cleaner than dark-skinned people.

The standard of beauty is based on White men's values. The closer a Black is to meeting those standards of the white man, the more desirable that person is.

WHAT'S YOUR WILLIE LYNCH?
WHATEVER IT IS,
LYNCH IT NOW!

SPECIAL THANKS

My first thanks goes to God, who gave me the talent to be able to write this book. He showed me the way to complete my book, when I didn't have any direction on how to finish. He provided the avenue for people to come into my life to help me.

I would also like to thank my very good friend Kenneth Morris. He pushed me to get this book finished. He gave me hope, when I sometimes didn't have it. He even baby-sitted the boys at times to give me a break. He kept me motivated. He stayed up a lot of nights with me and sacrificed his own responsibilities. He also did the First illustration, (what a man) but Chris Eubuehi did this version on the book . Much love to Belinda Pittman, who proof-read and edited my book. Chantal Hathman, my supportive friend who came over at night to help me type and edit. My wonderful neighbor, Patsy Medley, who offered so much inspiration and words from the Lord. My parents who backed me all the way, when I told them I wanted to publish my book. Most of all thank you Landon and Lance (my sons) for being patient with mommie. Some notable people I can't forget to thank for some of their input: Renee Dobson, (Aunt Nae Nae who is my Tanika) Londa Parks, (my save and delete buddy) Bill Golden, Anita Collins (my computer buddy) and Pat Burns. I can't forget Milton Henry my buddy, who gave me a free trip to Antigua where I finished most of the book. (Our friend JoAnn Swain was there with us). My cousin, Christina Richardson whose AKA used to be Tanika(ha ha!) And last but not least, my dearest friend in Arlington, TX Attorney Ingrid Stamps (Ryan her son). Last but not least Anwer Khan and Ali Mazhar from A-1 Printing & Graphics.

Note: This story is fictional. Any similarities to persons, places or events are not real. The Million Man's March took place October 16, 1995. Dates were changed to coincide, with the season and scenery of this story.

You can order this book online by accessing: Amazon.Com, Borders.Com and Barnes and Noble.Com

or send $11.00 +$3.20 shipping and handling to:
P.O. Box 1304
Gardena, CA 90249